Freedom First, Peace Later
By: Jeanette Hewitt
ISBN: 978-1-877546-48-8

Bluewood Publishing Ltd
Christchurch, 8441, New Zealand
www.bluewoodpublishing.com

Special Note: This book contains UK Spellings.

For more books published by Bluewood Publishing Ltd visit

www.BluewoodPublishing.com

Freedom First, Peace Later

by

Jeanette Hewitt

Dedication

This special book is dedicated to the memory of my grandmothers; Daisy Wozny and Ivy Hewitt, both avid readers who would have enjoyed my tale.

Huge thanks to my parents, Janet and Keith, who have encouraged me to follow my heart and have always supported me in any decisions I made. Thanks also to the support from my fiancé, Darren, and my family and friends.

Also thank you to Danny Morrison from the Bobby Sands Trust for providing me with information regarding the late Bobby Sands.

Thanks to all those people over the years who read my work and a final thank you to those who read this book and enjoy it – I ask for no more than that!

Chapter One

Stu

He was a soldier who felt like he wasn't sure what he was doing, that he had stumbled into this life on some form of pretence. Now, as he sat looking at the order he had received from his superiors, he felt that his last two years in the army had been spent playing at being a soldier, much like he had when he was a child. Oh, of course he had passed all of the tests – the physical and the mental, the exams and trials – but putting it into practice was a whole new ballgame, one that he had not yet had to face. It was not a great way to sell himself, he knew that, which is why he tried desperately to keep his head down and avoid looking ignorant. So far it had not been difficult; he had been based in London during his first year in the army. As a fresh faced eager sixteen-year-old it had been exciting, being away from home, just training, getting fit, learning the drill. The second year of his army career was spent in Bradford, which was great, because it meant that he could go home most weekends to see his family and mates.

Now, he sat on his bunk and read through the papers in his hand. The bitter taste of dread filled his mouth, and for a moment he feared he was going to be sick. He closed his eyes and breathed deeply for a few minutes before he looked once again at the file, reading over and over again the papers that were responsible for his panic.

A seven-month operational tour of Northern Ireland, which was to begin in the second week of December 1980, stationed in a camp in a town called Crossmaglen, about eighty miles south of Belfast.

1

He didn't know anything at all about the town, indeed, he had never even heard of Crossmaglen. Just the thought of Northern Ireland was enough to scare him – its reputation preceded it. When he had begun his army training the likelihood of being deployed to Northern Ireland was a high possibility and the conflict had been explained to Stu and his classmates. They were told in the briefest of terms that the two main communities' were Catholics and Protestants. Most Catholics considered themselves to be Irish and were Nationalist in their political outlook, which meant they would like to see the whole nation, including Southern Ireland, reunited and independent of Britain. Most Protestants however, considered themselves to be British and were Unionist in their political views therefore, they wanted Northern Ireland to remain part of the United Kingdom.

As Stu lay back on his bunk, he fingered the papers in his hand and breathed deeply. Maybe it wouldn't be so bad? After all, if he had not heard of Crossmaglen, perhaps it wasn't in the forefront of the fighting that dominated the news so much.

The door swung open and an older soldier, Richard Byrnes, strode in and over to his bunk.

"Rick, you've spent time in Ireland. Do you know anything about Crossmaglen?" asked Stu.

Rick, his back towards Stu, stiffened noticeably before he turned to face him.

"Why?" he asked, frowning.

Stu waved his papers in the air. "They're sending me there…"

Rick leaned back against his own bunk.

"It's rough man," he said eventually. "It's mainly Catholics in Crossmaglen and they hate us. They hate the Protestants too, which is why there's not many living there, although there's enough of them to spell constant trouble."

He held his hand out for Stu's order papers and glanced through them. "The camp is small, it only takes about seventy soldiers." He looked up at Stu, who was pale-faced and silent. "You'll be fine mate."

Stu nodded and took back his papers, leaning back on his bunk. He had a feeling that the relatively easy life of London and Bradford would be a distant memory. He would spend three quarters of the next year in Northern Ireland, and when he returned to England he would most likely be a changed man. In Ireland he would face hatred, based purely on his nationality and his job. As a blue-collar white boy, he had never faced racism or prejudice. As an army soldier, he had never yet killed, and the question he asked himself was could he?

* * * *

Bronwyn

Many miles away, across the Irish Sea, twenty-one year-old Bronwyn Ranger was getting ready for a night on the town. It was Saturday night, and even though there had been a curfew placed on her hometown of Crossmaglen, Bronwyn knew the places to go where folks scoffed at the word 'curfew'. She was waiting for her boyfriend, Danny Adams, to collect her. She swore softly as she glanced at her watch and saw that he was already half an hour late. Turning to her mirror, she appraised her reflection. Bronwyn was tall, almost six feet, and with her long, black hair and dark brown eyes she had no trouble charming the men in the area. But, Danny Adams had been the prize that she had bagged after a lot of hard work. It had been difficult because he had known her since childhood, was her

3

brother's best friend in fact, and, being four years older than she, it had taken a lot of effort on Bronwyn's part to get him to look in her direction. But finally she had snagged him, and now they had been together for a year.

Suddenly her pager beeped and she snatched it up. Danny's name flashed up on the screen and she cursed under her breath. It was a secret code that Bronwyn knew well and, picking up her leather jacket while mumbling crossly, she left the house.

Walking down the street, she slowed her step and looked around. This town she had lived in her whole life had been the setting for a lot of heartache and fighting, and all of a sudden the troubles seemed to have taken their toll. She had never noticed before how *grey* it was around here. From the buildings right down to the cobbles there was an air of oppression that seemed to hang over the streets like a fog. Her footsteps echoed eerily, and though Bronwyn had never been one to think too long or hard about her future, for a moment the drab land that surrounded her caught up with her, and, for a single heartbeat, she was suddenly very frightened. Not in the physical sense of who might be lurking in the cold, grey streets, but of what was to become, not just of her, but of her family, her friends, and even her country. She shook her head, long hair flying as though it could shake off both the fog and the thoughts, and she picked up her step as she broke into a run down to the phone box at the bottom of her street.

With a fervent glance around, she stepped inside and immediately put her hands on top of the telephone. Moving her fingers, she skimmed her hands lightly over the top of the phone, moved them down the sides and underneath. She turned in a 360-degree circle and, when she was satisfied she was alone, she squatted down and peered underneath the telephone that hung on the wall of the phone box. Her job done, she straightened up and leaned against the cold glass, watching her breath steam up the window while she waited, counting silently in her head. Before she reached thirty, the phone rang and she picked it up.

"Dan?" she said.

"Hey, babe, I'm not going to make it tonight," said a voice from the other end.

"Shit, Danny! One of these days I'm going to—" she broke off without finishing her sentence.

There was no use threatening him. Danny knew as well as she did that she was never going to carry out any of her threats after she had tried so hard to get him in the first place.

"I'll make it up to you, babe," he said.

"I know," she sighed and twisted the phone cord round her fingers. "Will I see you tomorrow?"

"I'll be along later tonight. I'll let myself in. Oh, and Bronwyn?"

"Yes?"

"I was with you all night, yeah?"

She sighed again and nodded into the phone. "It goes without saying, Dan."

After he had hung up, she stood in the phone box for a while before heaving the door open and looking out into the night. Now, her evening was ruined. She couldn't even go out to meet her mates in case her alibi was ever needed and somebody was to see her without Danny.

"Shit!" she hissed and stomped back along the cobbled street up to her house.

Chapter Two

Barry

When Bronwyn had turned into the gate of her house, a young man stepped out of the shadows near the phone box and glanced up the street. He lit a cigarette, and for a moment the glow of the match illuminated his face in the moonlight. Anybody watching at that moment could not fail to notice that he was Bronwyn's twin brother. Although they were fraternal twins, the physical similarities between Bronwyn and Barry Ranger were endless. Same jet-black hair, same height, same shape faces and features. But that was where the likeness ended. Barry was calm, while Bronwyn lived her life in the fast lane. Barry was quiet, while you always knew if Bronwyn was in the vicinity. But, different or not, they loved each other fiercely, and knew all of each other's secrets. Or so they thought…Bronwyn had no idea that Barry was an agent for the British government, pretending to be an integral member of the I.R.A, while all the time reporting their plans and movements back to his bosses. Barry had only been an agent for a year, but he had been involved long before it became official. How it happened was a common enough story; a man had approached Barry while he had been hanging around the corner shop one day, back when Barry had only been seventeen. The man, who called himself Johnny, had dropped hints about the kind of work he was in, and how beneficial—money wise—it could be for Barry. Just one glance at Johnny had proven how profitable this job could be with his Rolex, his sharp designer suit, and the seemingly never ending bank roll of notes that appeared out of his pocket. Being brought up on the breadline, the thought of spare cash that he wouldn't normally have made Barry agree to the requests that Johnny had. And oh, what easy money it had been at first. Listening to the men down at the social club or the guys that chatted easily about their work on the street corners where Barry spent most of his time. Nobody took any notice of a boy like him; being Bronwyn's brother he was used to blending into the background, and he found he had a skill for picking up information that he could take back to Johnny.

That was where it had started, and now Barry was in deep. As soon as he turned twenty, they offered him the role of an agent. There were many benefits, among them the money and easy hours. But, there was always the constant threat of being found out by his fellow I.R.A members. And Barry knew that if that day ever came, he would, quite literally, be a dead man.

The group, or cell as it was commonly called, that Barry was a part of consisted of four other members. They were a mixed group. There was Andy, the cell leader, a girl in her mid twenties called Kay, and two men of around Barry's age, Kian and Jones. Outside the I.R.A they were good men, men that Barry would have shared a pint with at the pub. But fraternising was not allowed. If they saw each other in the street they would not acknowledge each other, it was too dangerous. Another thing that Bronwyn was not aware that he knew was that her boyfriend Danny was a member of the I.R.A. This had been the biggest surprise going in undercover; a shocking discovery that had nearly made him quit the job as well. And the time that Barry had been dreading had arrived, his link to Danny had been discovered, and they had asked Barry to find out information about Danny's plans, as well as keeping them informed about his own cell. So far, he had discovered nothing, which was good news for Danny and good news for him. For, if the truth be told, Barry didn't want to have to tell on Danny. After growing up with him, and being in such close fraternity since he was now seeing Bronwyn, he loved Danny like a brother.

And the realisation that he could not put off the inevitable forever was devastating.

When Barry arrived home, he poked his head around the living room door and called out a greeting. His mother, Alia, and Bronwyn were huddled on the sofa watching the television.

"Barry!" Alia waved him in. "Come sit with us and take a cup of tea, won't you?"

He shrugged and came into the lounge, throwing a halfhearted greeting at Bronwyn.

"Hey, bro," she said and turned back to the television.

"No Danny tonight?" he asked.

"He's upstairs sleeping," Bronwyn lied without batting an eyelid. "Don't disturb him."

Barry gaped at his sister and her blatant lie. How did she have the nerve? She should have been an agent herself for sure; she could fool everyone with her acting abilities.

Barry sat down heavily in the armchair opposite Bronwyn and studied her. For all of their life they had confided in each other and shared everything. Now, on the brink of adulthood, she knew nothing about him, and it saddened him.

She sensed him staring and she turned to face him.

"What?" she snapped.

He stood up.

"Nothing. I think I'll turn in. Night all."

"Don't wake Dan!" she called as he left the room.

He didn't reply.

* * * *

Rosina

Across town, Bronwyn's best friend, Rosina James, was also up to her eyeballs in a lie. For six months now she had been seeing a lad, Connor Dean. There was a huge problem with that since Rosina was Catholic and Connor was Protestant. They say you cannot help with whom you fall in love, and for these two it was certainly true. And now, as Rosina hurried through the dark streets, head low and glancing around lest anybody should see her, she wondered whether she was doing the right thing.

"But you always wonder that," she muttered to herself as she turned down an alley to cut through to the Protestant side of town. "And you keep on bloody doing it anyway."

She hated walking through these streets alone to meet him, but would never tell Connor how much she dreaded the walk to his side of town. It always started when she left her house. She felt that with every step she took, one more person looked out of their window or poked their head out of their front door, until eventually it seemed that the whole of her neighbourhood were falling into step behind her, knowing what she was doing, where she was going, who she was seeing. When she reached Connor, invariably she was a nervous wreck, and she had always convinced herself that this was it, this was the *last time.* But then she would see him – Connor standing in the shadows, his handsome face half hidden in the moonlight, seemingly lost in his own thoughts, until she made her presence known and then his face would light up at the sight of her, and she knew never, ever could she leave him, no matter what the risks.

It happened now, as she came out onto Grosvenor Street and saw him sitting on the wall of one of the back gardens. He jumped down and waved and she stepped up her pace and waved back, her heart beating ever faster and a ridiculous grin on her face.

Suddenly, she stopped. Three men had appeared out of the shadows behind Connor. They wore black ski masks and she knew, even though she couldn't identify them, that they were from her side of town. Before Connor even realised that they were there, she knew what was going to happen.

She stalled; her whole body froze for a split second, as the dangers of intervening splintered through her brain, before her heart kick-started her legs into gear and she broke into a run.

"No!" She yelled and a look of confusion came over Connor's face before it was replaced by shock, then anger as he was knocked to the ground by one of the men. The third man ran towards Rosina and, as she attempted to dodge past him, he caught hold of her and swung her around to hold her in a vice-like grip as she cried out in fear.

"You watch this, Rosina James, and then you tell me if you wanna get involved with Protestant pig shit again," he breathed into her ear and gripped her chin, forcing her to watch the spectacle unfolding in front of her.

"Face down!" yelled the man holding Connor, and Rosina moaned in helpless terror as she saw the shotgun in his hand.

A dreadful howl rang through the silent night as a bullet ripped through the back of Connor's knee. Rosina honestly didn't know if it were her or Connor who had screamed so terribly.

"You fuckin' leave our lasses alone," hissed the man into Connor's ear.

He stood up, and turned towards Rosina.

"Keep a hold of her," he said menacingly and aimed a kick at Connor's inert body.

"Please, stop," sobbed Rosina and, twisting out of the man's grasp, she aimed her foot high like Bronwyn had taught her, catching the lad where it hurt him most with her boot.

He released his grip on her as he doubled over in pain, and, seeing her window of opportunity, she sprinted off down the street. She heard a yell and cursing behind her, but it only spurred her on as she ripped through the gardens and back alleys she had come to know so well. Over garden walls she leapt, not daring to stop, almost feeling the breath of her pursuers on the back of her neck, tearing through the washing that hung on the lines, not caring when she got caught up and it trailed across the gardens behind her. She was literally running for her life.

Finally, Rosina stopped running and slumped to the ground behind a dustbin. Tears stung her eyes and she heaved as the horror of what had happened replayed in her mind. Those bastards! He was just a man, just like them. Their relationship was nothing to do with anyone else and it was so unfair. She sat up straight as the enormity of the incident hit her.

Connor had been *shot!*

And she knew the way it worked, he would have been left there, in the road, all of the time losing more blood.

She pushed herself up and staggered back to the fence that she had just hurled herself over. No longer having any regard for her own safety, she started to make her way back to Grosvenor Street.

A curtain twitched and a pool of light fell onto the street where the three lads were working Connor over.

Curtain twitching was not an uncommon occurrence, and the person who dared to look normally did not approach them, even if it were one of their own kind. But this time the twitching curtain belonged to Connor's mother, Mary, and as she realised that it was her boy on the cobblestones she let out a strangled cry. Memories of another incident in another time pulsed through her head as she struggled with the catch, bubbling up inside her, crushing her thudding heart in her chest. At the same time as the window flew open the emotions tore up her throat and, with no words forming in her mind, she leaned out of the window and screamed hard and long into the night.

The three men simultaneously looked up and paused. Mary continued to scream, and her inability to find her power of speech eventually frightened her into silence. For a long moment they looked at each other, then, as Connor rolled over and raised his head, they all looked down at him.

"Ma! Don't you come out here," he tried to shout, but it came out as a whisper.

Mary Dean didn't even hear her son's warning; all that mattered was stopping the three men before they killed him. The man who held the shotgun appraised the situation rapidly. He seemed to decide that the woman in the window was no threat and turned back to the task at hand. Mary, shocked to her core by the past memory that mingled into the present day, was paralysed by fear. The lad who moved back to Connor was all she needed to make her body obey the commands that her brain was issuing and, without hesitating, she heaved herself up onto the window ledge and swung her legs over. As if they were encouraged by Mary's bravery, several more windows opened in the neighbouring houses. The three men looked at each other, knowing it was time to leave.

Their work done anyway, they melted away into the night as Mary hurried over to Connor.

By the time one of the neighbours had called for an ambulance, the three perpetrators were streets away, almost onto their homeland. They stopped at the Divide and silently shook hands before going their separate ways.

When his two accomplices had vanished into the darkness, Danny Adams pulled the ski mask off his face and threw it over a garden wall. Trying not to think of the lad that they had probably crippled for life, he made his way through the back streets to Bronwyn's house.

When Danny climbed into Bronwyn's bed, she stirred in her sleep.

"It's only me," he whispered.

"Danny?" she murmured and leaned over to switch on the light.

She blinked as her eyes became accustomed to the light and reached out to touch his face.

"You've got blood on your face," she stated.

He looked at her fingers, which were indeed bloodstained.

"Shit," he said softly, and got back out of bed.

Bronwyn lay down and listened to him in the bathroom.

A thousand questions ran through her head. Where had he been? Who had he been with? And whom had he hurt? But she would never ask him, and he would never tell her.

When they had been together for about three months, she had discovered that he was a follower of the I.R.A. They had been in the pub for about an hour when a man who was unknown to Bronwyn came up to Danny and beckoned him outside. Bronwyn, naturally curious, had followed and leaned against the doorframe as she listened to a conversation that, at the time, didn't interest her much. They appeared to be discussing an event in Warrenpoint a town in South Down. The two men were animated and speaking in hushed tones and Bronwyn, rapidly losing interest and feeling the chill of the late October air, wandered back inside.

She thought no more of what she had heard until, around ten days later, she came home from town and found her mother, Alia, sitting in the lounge, her attention focused on the television.

"What you watching Ma?" asked Bronwyn as she stuck her head round the door.

"News," replied Alia, and the catch in her voice made Bronwyn venture further into the room where she studied the television.

The news reporter's words as he outlined the story chilled Bronwyn.

"At least eighteen soldiers have been killed in two booby-trap bomb attacks at Warrenpoint. It is the highest death toll suffered by the British Army in a single incident since it arrived in Northern Ireland to restore order. The IRA are believed to be behind the attack."

"Warrenpoint…" Bronwyn rolled the word around her tongue trying to remember where she had heard it recently. A blush stained her cheeks and she froze as she remembered the conversation that she had heard between Danny and the stranger outside the pub. Without further word to Alia she had turned tail and fled, never mentioning it to anybody.

Bronwyn, not knowing much about the politics of the land she lived in, knew only of the fearsome reputation of the I.R.A and, when she had told Danny that she knew he had been involved in Enniskillen, she begged him not to get in any deeper. He had sat her down and told her not to worry, he knew what he was doing, and if it was something he believed in, then how could it not be right? Bronwyn listened as he told her about the activities of the I.R.A, and he made it sound okay. Yes, the things they did to civilians were bad, but, Danny assured her, they were justified. So, when he became a fully-fledged member, Bronwyn found herself covering for him.

When Danny returned to the bedroom, Bronwyn had turned the light out and was feigning sleep. Danny heaved a sigh and crawled in beside her. They lay together for the rest of the night, back to back, both awake, both lost in their own thoughts and fears.

Chapter Three

The Hospital

Rosina was still two streets away when the glow of flashing blue lights fell upon her, creating long blue shadows that faded in and out over the cobbles. She quickened her step until she arrived back at the spot where Connor had been shot and stared aghast at the crowd of people surrounding the ambulance. For a moment she hesitated, knowing that these people would all know Connor had been hurt because of her, but also knowing she couldn't leave him alone any longer, already she felt crushed that she had run away. Slowly, trying not to draw attention to herself she skirted around the crowd until she realised she was never going to make it through the throng of people. With tears streaming down her face, she elbowed her way through the crowds of neighbours that had gathered and, as Connor was being lifted into the ambulance, she ran up to the door.

He had an oxygen mask on, and his face was a mass of blood. A virtual river of blood from his leg left a trail as he was moved into the ambulance and, for a heart-stopping second, she thought that he was dead. But then she saw that his eyes were open, and as he saw her frightened face at the door of the ambulance, he held out his hand to her.

"Connor!" she cried and began to climb up into the ambulance.

"You get away from him!" A tall lady came around the side of the ambulance and pushed Rosina away. "You're the cause of this!"

"Mam, please…" Connor took the oxygen mask off his face and called out to his mother. "Leave her alone."

Mary glanced at her son and looked back at Rosina.

For a moment the two stared at each other before Mary broke the silence.

"Are you coming with us?" she asked quietly.

Rosina hesitated and looked around the sea of faces that crowded around the ambulance.

"If you don't, this lot are likely to lynch you, so they are," stated Mary.

Rosina nodded, and with a last glance into the unfriendly crowd she hauled herself up into the ambulance.

The ride to the hospital was fraught with tension. Rosina sat beside Mary, silent tears rolling down her cheeks. Connor slipped in and out of consciousness while the paramedics worked, fixing drips to him.

At the hospital, Mary and Rosina were left alone in a side room while they took Connor into theatre.

"How long have you been with him?" Mary asked in her thick Irish brogue.

"Six months." Rosina stared down at the carpet.

Mary watched Rosina quietly for a while, interested in what must be so special about this girl that her usually levelheaded son would risk his life for. The girl, although pretty, reminded her of a field mouse, shaking and unable to meet Mary's eye.

"Connor's dad was a Catholic," said Mary, and Rosina looked up in surprise.

"I didn't know that," she said. "Isn't he—?"

"Dead. Yes, that he is." Mary looked Rosina straight in the eye. "Killed by your lot."

Rosina looked back down to the floor at Mary's words.

"I was nearly run out of town," Mary carried on with her story. "But I stuck it out, raised my boy, worked hard and finally got back a little of the respect I had before."

"I'm sorry," said Rosina.

"But, could you stick it, girl?" Mary's eyes glinted in the dim light of the room. "Sitting there, looking like a deer caught in the headlights, looking like you wouldn't say *boo* to a goose. If your family threw you out and your friends spat at you in the street, could you handle it?"

Rosina raised her head and met Mary's gaze head on.

"I could. I love your son, Mrs Dean, and I'll give up anything for him. We'll move away from here to somewhere where stupid politics don't matter. I *can* handle it."

Mary laughed; a harsh, brittle sound without any humour.

"We'll see, girl. We'll see how long you stick around, now the truth is out."

It was dawn when Rosina left the hospital. When news had come from the operating theatre that Connor was going to be okay, she made her promises to Mary that she would return that evening.

Mary had not commented, instead she simply raised an eyebrow in a way that made her look like she knew better, and smirked. The girl had no backbone. No way would she be able to face everything that the community was going to throw at her.

Now, Rosina didn't know where to go. Home was an option that she could not yet face. News would have spread, and she couldn't face her mother. Not yet.

As she stood at the bus shelter the bus trundled into view, and she smiled. During times of trouble there was only one place to go.

Bronwyn's.

Bronwyn had just drifted off to sleep when someone hammered on the front door. She opened her eyes and looked over at Danny who was still sleeping soundly.

"Ma?" she called. "Barry?"

There was a second knock at the door and a flurry of swearing from her mother's room. Bronwyn sighed and snuggled down further into her duvet. Sleep was almost upon her again when her mother hollered up to her.

"Bronwyn!"

Grumbling to herself and clambering over Danny, she reached for her dressing gown and made her way downstairs.

Alia hurried back upstairs, shooting Bronwyn a look as she passed.

"Rosie!" Bronwyn took one look at her tear-streaked face and drew her into the kitchen. "What in hell has happened to you?"

"Oh, Bronwyn." Rosina's lip trembled and she threw her arms round her friend.

"Rosie, come on and sit down. Tell me what's happened."

Rosina shook her head and tried to pull herself together.

"I was meeting Connor last night, and just as I got to where we were meeting he was jumped by some lads. They grabbed me, they made me watch…" Rosina broke off as tears threatened again.

"Christ alive! Did they hurt you?" Bronwyn demanded.

"No, I got away. But they had a…a…" as the memory came rushing back Rosina clapped a hand to her mouth. "Gonna be sick!" she squeaked.

Bronwyn hauled Rosina over to the sink and rubbed her friend's back as she heaved. When Rosina was spent she led her back to the chair.

"What did they do, Rosie?" she asked softly.

"They shot him," Rosina spoke in a whisper and closed her eyes. "His... in his..." she was unable to finish her words but Bronwyn knew all too well what she was trying to say.

"Kneecapped?" Bronwyn covered her face with her hands. "My God, Rosie, one leg or both?"

"One. But it's bad enough. I spent the night at the hospital with him," replied Rosina.

Before Bronwyn could ask any more, Barry came into the kitchen.

"Hey, what's all the noise? Oh hey, Rosie, Jeez what happened to you?"

As she busied herself making tea, Bronwyn recounted the story to Barry. His face darkened as he heard what the men had done.

"Fucking monsters," he muttered. "But Rosie, what were you thinking of getting involved with one of *them*?"

"It shouldn't matter!" wailed Rosina. "It's nobody else's business anyway."

"Did you recognise any of them? And how did they find out?" Barry fired questions at her.

"I don't know. Bronwyn's the only person I've told about us. They must have followed me one night."

Barry turned to his sister.

"And you didn't tell anyone?"

"No!" she snapped.

But that wasn't strictly true. Pieces of information began to click into place in her mind like a jigsaw. She had confided in Danny. Danny was in the I.R.A, the organisation that opposed mixed relationships. Danny had cancelled their date last night to do something that obviously involved the I.R.A. Finally, Danny had returned late, covered in somebody else's blood.

A flush spread over Bronwyn's face and she turned to the kettle to hide her face. Oh, it couldn't be true. Danny wouldn't do that to her best friend.

Would he?

Before she could think further, Danny wandered into the kitchen. He stopped short when he saw Rosina, and Bronwyn noted the look that came over his face before he recovered his composure.

It was a look of panic and fear. It was a look of guilt.

"Hey, Rose," said Danny casually. "How you doin'?"

Bronwyn slammed the kettle down.

"How does it look like she's doing?" she snapped. "And we were having a private conversation until the world and his wife interrupted. Can you all piss off and leave us alone!"

Three faces looked at her in surprise at her outburst.

"Well, if it's private don't do it in public," retorted Barry and turned to Danny. "Fancy heading over to the pub for breakfast?"

Danny pulled his gaze away from Rosina and nodded.

Without another word, he left the room.

"Sorry about that," said Bronwyn and put a mug of tea down in front of Rosina.

"That's okay," Rosina sighed. "You don't know how lucky you are, Bron. Not only can you see your guy out in the open, your ma even lets him stay over—in your bed!"

"Oh, well the last part is easy. When I started seeing Dan, my ma knew I'd be for shagging him anywhere. 'Better under my roof, where I know where you are!'" Bronwyn did a passable impersonation of Alia, and it at least raised a smile from Rosina.

They sat in companionable silence for a while until Bronwyn spoke again.

"So, what now?" she asked.

Rosina drained the mug of tea and stood up.

"I guess I better face the music at home."

Later that day Bronwyn caught up with Danny.

He hadn't moved after breakfast in the Fox and Hound, and Bronwyn noted with distaste that he was drunk.

"I want to talk to you," she said as she slid into the booth and sat down opposite him. "Tell me it wasn't you did that to Connor last night."

He regarded her seriously and shook his head.

"It wasn't me who did that to Connor last night."

"Bullshit!" she exploded. "I'm not an idiot. I saw the look on your face when you saw Rosina this morning."

Danny slammed his pint glass down on the table, making her jump.

"Well, what do you want me to say? If you already know, why the hell are you asking me?"

Bronwyn covered her face with her hands.

"I love you, Danny," she said. "But I love Rosina too. She's my best friend and you made her watch while you shot Connor."

"It's my job," replied Danny coldly.

Bronwyn was lost for words. Danny was no good; no matter what cause he believed in, it didn't justify shooting a lad who was only guilty of seeing a girl from the wrong side of the track. But she loved him, purely and simply, and that was hard to forget, no matter what he did.

She sat back and looked around the smoky pub where she worked four nights a week. It was like a second home to her, and she knew everybody in here by name, indeed had known them all of her life. How many of the men in here were also in the I.R.A? Men she had grown up with and looked up to. How many others led a double life?

"It's not right," she said quietly.

"Oh, for fuck's sake, Bronwyn, grow up." Danny drank the last of his pint.

"I try to understand, but I can't," she cried. "You're the only person in my life who is connected to that stupid gang, and I can't get my head around your reasons. Connor and Rosie are good people, *decent* people."

He leaned in so close she smelt the beer on him.

"I'm not the only one involved, Bronwyn—try looking closer to home," he spoke quietly and stood up.

She grabbed his arm as he walked past.

"What? Who are you talking about? Tell me!" she said angrily but he shook her hand off and stalked out of the pub.

Grabbing her coat, she ran after him and caught hold of him.

"Don't walk away from me! What did you mean just now?"

He pushed her away and she stumbled and sat down hard on the pavement.

"Barry isn't so righteous after all, sweetheart. Throw some of your patronising bullshit his way."

Lost for words, Bronwyn sat and gaped open-mouthed as Danny walked away.

This time she didn't follow him.

* * * *

It looked like World War Three had broken out on Rosina's street. She groaned inwardly as she saw a cluster of women gathered around her house, her mother standing in the centre of them.

She stopped and glanced around. Her blood turned cold at what she saw.

The young kids in the street stared at her, footballs abandoned as a real life rebel walked in their midst. The older kids edged closer to her and she stared in shock as a great gob of spit landed on her shoe.

Being a black sheep was new to Rosina. Raised single-handedly by a mother who ruled with a rod of steel, she had spent her whole life playing by the rules. Never had she given her mother a moment of trouble or worry and, unlike Bronwyn, she had never shoplifted, skipped school, or been in trouble with the law. She had never given anyone cause to chastise her. Until now.

"Traitor!" shouted someone and the yell made her mother look up.

For a moment they stared at each other, until Rosina hung her head and started walking again towards the house.

The women parted like the Red Sea and allowed her through until she stood face to face with her mother, Kathleen.

Kathleen's hand came out and gripped Rosina's arm, and in one fluid movement, she was pulled into the house.

Kathleen slammed the door shut and turned to face her daughter.

"Mam—"

Kathleen slapped Rosina's face. Hard.

Tears sprang to Rosina's eyes as she clasped her hand to her cheek.

"How could you?" Kathleen's face was ablaze with fury. "Why couldn't you stick to your own?"

Rosina trembled at her mother's wrath and wished desperately that she could be more like Bronwyn. Bronwyn would just tell Kathleen to fuck off.

"He's just a friend," Rosina whispered and instantly despised herself for not sticking up for Connor and lying about their relationship.

"That's a lie!" Kathleen roared as Rosina covered her face with her hands and turned to the wall.

"Mam, please!" Rosina was openly crying now, which seemed to make Kathleen even angrier.

"A Protestant pig! My daughter and a pig. I'm a laughing stock! My neighbours, who always respected me, are laughing at me!" Kathleen shouted.

Suddenly, something in Rosina snapped and she spun around. She had never felt anything like the fury that boiled up inside her, and she stormed back towards her mother until they were face to face.

"I was hurt last night, Ma. A man grabbed me and they made me watch while they shot Connor in his leg. Then they left him on the ground and came after me. I had to run away, I had to hide because I was so frightened and I was all alone out there. And you're worried about your *neighbours*? You're worried that people are *laughing*?" Rosina shrieked. "What about me? What about your daughter? I could have been shot or raped..." she tailed off and slumped against the wall. "And you don't care."

Ashen faced, Kathleen seemed paralysed by Rosina's outburst. Before she could respond, Rosina walked back to the door. As she opened it, she turned around.

"I'm going to visit my boyfriend in the hospital," she said and pulled the door open wide.

The crowd that were gathered looked up as Rosina strode down the path, and this time she walked with her head held high. The group sensed her determination and they let her through. When she got to the end of the road she heard her mother's high pitched voice cutting through the crows behind her.

"Don't you come back here!" Kathleen shrieked. "If you see him, you're not welcome in my house!"

"Fine," said Rosina quietly without turning around.

As she walked briskly back in the direction of the hospital she smiled through her tears. All of her life she had tried to pretend that her mother loved her, that her actions were simply that of a strict mother. Now she knew it was not true. There was no love between them, and all of a sudden she felt lighter somehow, as though a great weight had been lifted off her shoulders. She had stood up to her mother for the first time in her life and it felt good. God, this must be how Bronwyn felt all of the time! And she *was* free now; free to do whatever she pleased. She could see Connor and take care of him. They would no longer have to hide their love. Picking up her pace, she hurried towards him, towards her future.

Chapter Four

Betrayals

Stu Jackson's bags were packed and he took a final look around the barracks that had served as his home. He wouldn't be seeing them again for a long time, but then, that was the life he had chosen, and although Northern Ireland wasn't his choice, at least he had a week at home to look forward to.

Or so he thought.

As he was about to call for a cab to the station, the Sergeant crashed through the door, startling Stu.

"Sorry, Jackson, leave's over. They need you guys in Crossmaglen now."

Stu's heart sank to the bottom of his boots.

"But, Sir—"

"No buts. Crossmaglen has been put on high alert and things are about to kick off. You're going over to Ireland with Carter and King. Truck leaves in twenty minutes."

With that the Sergeant left and Stu dropped his bag, aiming a kick at it in disgust.

"Bad luck, mate," said Mitchell, a fellow soldier who had not been put on the Northern Ireland trip.

His tone was tone half-sympathetic, half-relieved that it wasn't him.

"This is horse shit!" said Stu. "Where's Carter?"

Mitchell shrugged and Stu opened the door into the yard to look for the other two who were supposed to be going with him.

Stu caught sight of Tommy Carter crossing the yard towards the barracks, with Sam King striding along beside him. They ran up to Stu and, by the look on the two men's faces, they were not too happy with this latest news either.

"I can't believe this! We're not supposed to be going yet. What's this all about?" asked Stu.

"I.R.A is acting up. Intelligence got news of some pretty heavy duty shit going down, so they're drafting more men in," replied Carter. "We're the first lot to be going, but they're taking soldiers from barracks all over the North."

"I had a week's leave," said Stu mournfully.

"Fuck your leave, I was supposed to be getting hitched in two days!" exclaimed Sam.

"Sorry, man," said Stu. "Who knows when we'll get home again?"

"I'll be thinking of you guys when I'm sunning myself on a beach in Cyprus!" they heard Mitchell guffawing from inside and the three exchanged glances.

"It'll be his turn one day," said Stu darkly. "Come on guys."

"Yeah, let's go," Tommy said, and together they walked down to wait for the truck which would take them into the unknown.

* * * *

When Barry arrived home after his cell meeting, he discovered the house in darkness and Bronwyn sitting alone in the lounge.

"Hey, what's up?" he asked as he flicked the light on.

He stopped short as he saw the look of pure thunder on Bronwyn's face.

"Sis?" he asked, his hand frozen at the light switch.

"How could you?" she said quietly. "How could you lie to me all this time?"

"I don't know what you mean—"

"Yes you do," she cut him off mid-sentence. "You're with the I.R.A, and that makes you part of what happened to Rosina last night."

Barry felt his face flush and he took a deep breath. This was what he had been frightened of – Bronwyn finding out about his secret life. He didn't want her thinking that he was in the I.R.A, but she couldn't find out that he was actually there undercover.

"It's no big deal," he said and moved over to the couch. "I'm not involved in any violence, that I swear to you."

She stood up and faced him.

"Everything about it stands for violence!"

"No, you have to believe me. I don't get involved in any of that. I've never done anything like what happened last night, and I never will. It was sick, what happened to Rosina," he protested.

Bronwyn looked confused.

"So, that means you don't believe in it fully. What sort of member does that make you?"

"It's not all black and white, Bron. There are grey areas too," he replied.

Bronwyn stared at him for a long moment before she turned and walked to the door. When she reached it, she turned around to face him again.

"I've never tried to change Danny's beliefs about this cause, I wouldn't try to change yours. But it hurts that you didn't tell me, and it hurts that you think so little of Rosina that you could support something that has maimed Connor for life."

With that she went out of the room and a moment later he heard the front door slam.

Many thoughts started to move through Barry's mind. Bronwyn had said that she never tried to change Danny's beliefs, which meant that she knew that he was a member of the I.R.A. This was something that totally shocked him; he had been certain that only he knew about Danny and his connection to the I.R.A. This made his job much harder, because if he ever had to grass on Danny, there was always a chance that Bronwyn may be involved as well.

When Bronwyn closed the door behind her, she stopped and shivered in the cold night air. Where to go now? She didn't want to go back inside and listen to more of Barry's lies. She didn't want to see Danny at the moment either. That just left Rosina. She pulled her coat tighter around her and ran to the telephone box down the road. Her hands shook with the cold as she dialed Rosina's home number. Eventually, Rosina's mother picked up.

"Hi, Mrs James, is Rosie there?"

"No, she's not, and she won't be coming back here."

Bronwyn stared dumbly at the receiver as she heard Kathleen slam the phone down.

Well, Rosina must have told her all about Connor. But, where had she gone? In times of trouble the two girls always went to each other, but obviously Rosina hadn't come to the house.

The hospital!

Bronwyn came out of the phone box and turned around just in time to see a bus turning the corner at the top of the road. She stepped off the curb and flagged it down, digging around in her pockets for the fare.

As Bronwyn was getting on the bus, Rosina had just made it to the hospital. Connor's mother looked surprised when Rosina came into the ward and she held her finger to her lips.

"He's asleep," she whispered and motioned for Rosina to follow her out of the room.

As they stood in the corridor, Mary looked Rosina up and down.

"Well, I didn't expect to see you again," she said.

Rosina said nothing and stared at the floor.

Mary sensed that Rosina had not had an easy time of it since leaving the hospital that morning and she felt a wave of sympathy for the girl.

"Was it very bad?" she asked softly.

Rosina looked up and Mary saw the tears in her eyes.

"My ma kicked me out. The kids spat on me and called me a traitor," she said in a small voice. "Just like you said they would."

"You could get out now," said Mary and turned away.

"Never!" the sudden strength in Rosina's voice startled Mary.

"It'll get worse," Mary said.

"What happened to your husband?"

The sudden change of subject caught Mary unaware and she turned back to Rosina.

"If you're serious about my boy, I guess you'll need to know what to expect. Hell, if I tell you, it'll probably make you run faster from this hospital than you did last night when you were being chased by them murdering bastards."

Rosina reached out and touched Mary's arm.

"Tell me."

Mary nodded and together they went into the relatives' room Mary had been given to use.

"Get us some coffee, girl, this is a long tale."

As Rosina fed money into the coffee machine, she listened intently as Mary began to talk.

Chapter Five

Mary's Story

Crossmaglen 1960.
New Years Eve.

The party was at a house in Hilltown. Mary, who had just celebrated her eighteenth birthday, had a date to the party. Bob was just a casual acquaintance; there was no chance of romance, but it didn't stop him hoping.

Just after eleven o'clock, a man came in. He was tall and his skin was dark; not Asian but the sort of hue that comes from working outside. He was the kind of man who made women give him a second glance, and when his gaze settled on Mary she blushed. He spoke with the host of the party briefly and just as he walked back out the front he turned back, sought out Mary, and flashed her a grin.

For the rest of the evening, Mary fought off Bob's attentions as she looked around in case the mystery man had returned. Then, just before midnight, she saw him, standing alone by the fireplace, his eyes fixed upon her. As if by some unspoken agreement, they moved towards each other as the countdown to midnight began.

"Happy New Year," he said.

"Yes," Mary replied foolishly, and then he kissed her.

It wasn't the kiss of two strangers wishing each other a Happy New Year. It was a kiss between lovers, and Mary pulled away, quite breathless.

"Who are you?" Mary asked, still in his arms but not wanting him to let go.

"Billy." He released her and held out a hand, which she shook solemnly.

"Mary."

"What do you say we leave this party, Mary?" he asked.

"But Bob..." She gestured to him and Billy cut her off.

"Bob will be fine," he said and took her hand.

She felt all eyes on her as she and Billy hurried to the front door.

Outside, Mary paused, not quite sure what to do. Billy took the lead however and, taking her hand, he led her down the drive, out into the road and down the hill away from the main streets of Hilltown. They spent most of the night walking and talking. They ended up at Kilkeel, sitting on the beach, not noticing how cold it was. Mary and Billy spent that night getting to know each other and, when the dawn broke over the sea, he kissed her again. At that moment, Mary, not normally one for fairytales and romance, knew that she had found her one true love. Until he told her he was Catholic.

The troubles in Ireland, although they'd been there for centuries, had started to escalate. Mary felt like someone had punched her hard in the stomach. She knew that if she were to stay with Billy, they would have to leave Crossmaglen, leave Northern Ireland altogether. As they spoke of this possibility neither of them were certain if they were ready for that. Their earlier carefree talk now took on a serious tone. By the time the sun had fully risen in the sky over the first day of 1968, they had a plan. They would keep their relationship quiet until they were sure of their love. And they followed the plan to the letter. For nine months, they met up several times a week and made plans for when they would leave Ireland. Billy had been to New York and, as he told Mary all about the city, she knew that was where they should start their new life. Separately they worked and never spent a single penny of what they earned, stashing it away in a savings account ready for when the time came to leave. Mary cashed in a life insurance policy. Billy did the same on his savings bonds. By the time September came, they had saved four thousand pounds. It was enough to make a fresh start and they planned to leave on October the 1st. It was Mary's job to get the tickets and one Saturday in the middle of September she went to the town centre. As she neared the travel agency she literally ran into her best friend, Meg. If they had looked up at that moment they would have seen the huge I.R.A mural behind them that warned every passer-by in bold, black letters:

Loose talk costs lives. In taxis. On the phone. In clubs and bars. At football matches. At home with friends. Anywhere! Whatever you say — say nothing!

However, they didn't look at anything except each other as they greeted each other with a hug. Now, Meg knew nothing about Mary's plans; she hadn't dared breathe a word about Billy to anybody yet, but now, when everything had gone so well for months, she pulled Meg into the travel agency. As the lady booked the flight to New York, in hushed tones she told Meg everything. Meg was at first concerned, well aware of the danger Mary and Billy had placed themselves in, but, as a best friend would, she hugged Mary and made her promise to stay in touch. In turn, Mary told her she must come over to New York to visit, and how much she would love Billy.

It was only as Mary held out her hand for the tickets that she realised the assistant had listened to everything Mary and Meg had discussed. The look on her face made Mary's blood run cold. The assistant looked disgusted, and didn't reply when Mary bade her goodbye. Mary narrowed her eyes and snatched her plane tickets from her, mentally cursing her for being such a bigot, and pledged to not let the woman spoil her day because it was a special day. That morning Mary had found out that she was pregnant and, as far as she was concerned, it was all that was needed to complete them as a couple.

But spoil Mary's day she did. In fact Mary would now go to say that the seemingly innocent assistant at the travel agent spoiled her entire life. That woman—Joanne was her name— immediately made some telephone calls and told some people very high up what she had heard in her little shop that day.

They were waiting for Billy when Mary went to meet him. Just like they were waiting for Connor twenty-one years later. They were different men, more than likely the fathers or uncles of the men that lay in wait for Connor and Rosina. In fact, it was so identical, it was ironic.

Rosina listened quietly as Mary relived her story and, when she stopped, Rosina leaned forward to take the empty coffee cup out of Mary's hand. She sensed not to push Mary into talking; she would resume when she was ready.

"More coffee?" she asked.

"Yes, yes, please." Mary pulled herself out of the past and into the present. "I didn't realise it would be so hard talking about it."

"Does Connor know? I mean, have you ever told him this?" asked Rosina as she retrieved two more coffees.

"He knows his dad was a Catholic, but no, he doesn't know what I've told you."

Rosina came back across the room and handed Mary her coffee.

They sat in silence for a long time before Mary began to talk again.

"We had arranged to meet at the shipyard in Crossmaglen, and it was almost midnight when I got there. The yard was deserted. It wasn't even used as a shipyard anymore so we were never disturbed there. I saw him at once, sitting on the wall of the dock, and I pulled the tickets out of my pocket and waved them at him. I saw his face light up and, as I got close to him, he stood up on the wall and was about to jump down when three men came out of the shadows behind the wall. I stopped, too scared even to shout, and as they pulled Billy off the wall and onto the ground behind it, I started to run to him. I had no thought for my own safety. I knew what was going to happen. I'd heard about the kneecappings and the shootings and I'd even seen the aftermath of one once a couple of years before. I knew that I couldn't stop them from hurting Billy, I just prayed as I ran to him that hurt him was all that they would do.

"They hauled him up as I reached the wall that separated us, and we all stood there like idiots. Two men were each holding one of Billy's arms, the third man just behind us, standing staring at them.

"'Run,' Billy urged me and I saw the despair in his eyes as I shook my head.

"'No, don't run. Stay and watch,' said one of the men, and as I stared into his eyes I had never felt such hatred before.

"Suddenly, they sprang into action. The man on Billy's left pulled out a handgun and, before I knew it, a shot rang out. The noise was loud, louder than anything I'd ever heard and I remember clamping my hands to my ears. It didn't block out the sound of Billy's screams as they cocked the hammer and pulled the trigger again. I couldn't see where they had shot him. The wall was in my way, but I prayed that it was his legs and not any vital organs. I looked directly at Billy, and his eyes locked on mine as he sagged against the two men who held him up.

"'Let him go now,' I pleaded.

"The two men holding Billy looked at each other. They nodded, and I could see that they were just about to release him when the third man stepped closer to Billy. He whispered something in his ear, something that I didn't hear, and suddenly Billy lurched forward, out of the grip of the two men and slumped over the wall. For a second I was confused, and then I saw the knife sticking out of Billy's back. I screamed and screamed, and, to my ears, my screaming sounded louder than the gunshots. I was hysterical. It seemed like hours later that I finally got a hold of myself and stopped screaming. The men had gone. It was just Billy and me. I stumbled over to him and fell to my knees in front of him.

"I called his name and slapped his face. Eventually, he opened his eyes and stared blearily at me.

"'It's all over, sweetheart,' he said quietly. On reflex I moved back, and a river of blood came out of Billy's mouth as he spoke.

"'I'll get help,' I said and stood up.

"It must have taken all of his strength to lift his hand and pull me back.

"'Too late,' he whispered. 'Stay with me.'

"Of course I knew that it was too late. He had two bullets in him, and a butcher's knife sticking out of his back. He didn't seem to be in too much pain, maybe he had passed that stage, but I knew that he was dying.

"I climbed over the wall and stood next to him. Looking back now, I can't believe that I was so calm, although maybe I realised that this was the last time we were ever going to be together. I couldn't waste it by getting hysterical.

"'Should I move you?' I asked.

"He shook his head, so I sat down on the ground and clutched his hand.

"'I love you, Billy,' I said and then I told him that we were going to have a baby.

"The light in his eyes had nearly faded, but when I told him that they lit up. He couldn't speak now, but he gripped my hand and I knew that he was as happy about the baby as I was.

"Minutes later his head fell forward and he died."

Mary sat with her head bent as Rosina stared, ashen-faced.

"What happened next?" she asked.

"I left him eventually and went to the police station. I told them what had happened, and two officers came with me back to the dock. They didn't talk to me, didn't offer any comfort or sympathy. They knew why he had been killed and that I was the reason."

Rosina felt a sob rise in her throat, and she clamped her hand to her mouth.

Mary glanced up and saw the look on Rosina's face.

"It's not all bad," she said. "I got Connor, didn't I?"

Rosina nodded, still not trusting herself to speak.

"That was hard, telling my mother about the pregnancy. She threw me out, of course. The day after Billy died, I found myself on the streets, homeless, penniless and pregnant. I got a refund on the tickets to America and went to see Meg. She was my rock," Mary broke off and smiled at Rosina. "She's still my best friend now. The only person who didn't desert me during those black days."

"You never met anyone else?" asked Rosina.

Mary laughed; a harsh, brittle sound that echoed around the small room.

"A single, Protestant mother with a dead Catholic's child? No, nobody would touch me after that." Catching the look of sympathy in Rosina's eyes she stood up. "And I didn't want anyone. I'd had my chance—my love. Anyway, I took Billy's name so a part of him and me are forever together. It's more than some people get. I was lucky."

"But you're…liked now?"

"I am." Mary held her head up. "I'm respected and I'm respectable. Or, at least I was, until you came along."

"But you must understand!" Rosina said desperately. "How I feel about Connor, surely *you*, of all people, must understand!"

Mary said nothing.

Rosina leaned back in her chair and thought about everything Mary had told her. She knew that it could get just as bad for Connor and herself. The question was, were they strong enough to handle it?

A nurse coming into the room interrupted her thoughts, and she stood up quickly.

"Mrs Dean, your son is awake and asking for you."

Mary nodded and, as she held the door, she turned back towards Rosina.

"Are you coming?"

Rosina's face broke into a smile and, for a heartbreaking second, Mary could see why Connor had fallen for this girl. She took a second to pray for them both, for the strength that they would need in the months and years ahead.

* * * *

"Hey!" Connor's eyes widened as Mary and Rosina walked into his room together. "This is a sight I didn't think I'd see."

Mary hugged Connor and kissed his forehead. She smiled at him for a moment before stepping back and letting Rosina up to the bed. She took his hand and kissed it before bursting into tears.

"Babe, it's okay. I'm all right, see?" Connor gripped her hand. She nodded and tried to get a hold of herself.

He looked terrible. His right eye was swollen closed, and he had stitches in his forehead, where he had received a vicious cut. Rosina sat on the edge of the bed, taking care not to touch his heavily bandaged leg.

"Girl's been kicked out of her home," said Mary as she sat down on the side of the bed.

Connor looked horrified.

"Does everyone know?" he asked his mother.

"Yes," Mary replied.

"What are you going to do?" He looked at Rosina but it was Mary who answered.

"What do you think she's going to do?" Mary pulled a tissue out of her bag and passed it over the bed to Rosina. "She's coming to stay with us."

* * * *

Barry sat quietly in the cell meeting, concentrating hard on what Andy was saying. The cell leader was planning an attack on a local Catholic off-license that had been caught serving out of hours to Protestants. It was vital that he remembered every piece of information Andy fed him so he could deliver it back to Johnny, the British government agent.

"So, Kay, you'll stash the weapons until the big night. Baz, you'll arrange transport. We'll need a car, preferably stolen, to drive up to the gates, and another vehicle to get away in," Andy finished and looked around the table at his fellow comrades.

"When are we doing this?" asked Barry.

Andy paused and looked again at each of the people seated. It seemed to Barry that Andy's gaze lingered a little too long on him, and he shifted nervously in his chair.

"Soon," Andy said finally.

The meeting finally broke up and the group members disappeared into the night. As Barry walked the mile or so back home, he couldn't help but think about Bronwyn. She had been shocked to discover his involvement in the I.R.A, but she would be devastated if she ever learned that he was just there undercover. Devastated, because she knew the dangers that he faced. The problem with being an agent was that the more attacks and killings and bombs that he stopped, the more likely he was to get caught. Sooner or later, Andy was going to realise that every job that got messed up was a job that Barry was involved in.

Barry rubbed his eyes as a faint headache started. He had another problem on his hands; he wasn't sleeping.

Well, he started off sleeping each night, but for the last week he had begun waking earlier and earlier to find it utterly impossible to drop off again. Last night he had tried going to bed later, and had stayed awake until just after midnight. But he had still woken at five o'clock. It was all the stress of this damn job, he told himself. But he was caught now. Caught in a trap between the Irish Republican Army and the British government, and, if the truth be told, he didn't entirely trust either one of them.

As Barry trudged slowly home, he noticed the bright light of an off-license across the street, ironically the one that they had just been planning to bomb. Already feeling a quart of whiskey warming up his belly, he crossed the road.

Well, it would at least help him sleep, if nothing else.

* * * *

Bronwyn located Connor's bed just after Mary had dropped the bombshell about Rosina staying at their house. She pulled back the curtain and appraised the serious faces around the bed.

"Bronwyn!" Rosina cried and stood up to greet her friend.

"Bronwyn, hey?" Connor smiled at the pretty dark haired girl and held out his hand to her. "Rosina's told me all about you. It's good to finally meet you."

Bronwyn studied the boy in the bed. Rosina had landed herself a right looker. He was quite dark skinned, and his hair matched the raven's colour of her own. He was very handsome and his smile melted her heart. She stepped forward and smacked his hand aside.

"From Rosie's guy I expect a hug not a handshake!" she said.

Connor's look of surprise made Rosina giggle and she pulled Bronwyn down onto a chair.

"I'm sorry it's under these circumstances that we finally meet," said Bronwyn and then turned to Mary. "Hello. Are you Connor's ma?"

Mary had watched this exchange with hidden amusement. She liked this Bronwyn girl on sight. She could tell immediately that she was tough as nails, a good person for Connor and Rosina to have rooting for them.

"That I am," she replied and stood up. "What say I get us all some coffee?"

The three youngsters murmured their agreement and silently watched Mary leave.

Bronwyn turned to Rosina.

"How did it go with your ma?"

Rosina was downcast.

"She threw me out, but Mary said I could stay with her and Connor."

"Fantastic!" said Bronwyn. "Now, Connor, when are you getting out of this shit hole?"

"As soon as I can stand again," replied Connor and pulled up the sheet so Bronwyn could peer at the bandage that adorned his leg.

"Bron, I need to ask a favour," said Rosina in a small voice. "I need some things…"

Bronwyn held up her hand.

"Say no more. I'll get your stuff and bring it round to Connor's. You just write me the address and it'll be there."

"You're the best friend a girl could ever ask for. But what about me mam?" said Rosina as she scribbled Connor's address down and handed it over.

Bronwyn took the paper and memorised the address before looking back up at Rosina.

"You just leave her to me," she said and planted a kiss on Connor's cheek. "See ya."

And with that, she enveloped Rosina in a fierce hug and was gone.

Connor looked perplexed.

"Does she always move that fast?"

Rosina sighed and stared after Bronwyn's departing figure.

"Always," she replied.

Outside the hospital, Bronwyn stood in the rain and tried to compose herself. It was the first time she had met Connor, and she could tell immediately that he was a good, decent lad. How could Danny have hurt him like that? And why had she shot her mouth off to him about Rosina and Connor? That surely made this mess partly her fault. She clenched the piece of paper with Connor's address on it tight in her fist and swallowed against the tears that threatened.

You're the best friend a girl could ever ask for.

Bronwyn snorted and headed off to the bus stop.

Oh, darling Rosie, if only you knew...

Chapter Six

Kathleen

It didn't take Bronwyn long to get to Rosina's house. She had known Kathleen James all of her life, and could easily see why Rosina was so scared of her mother. But Bronwyn was not Rosina, and, as she rapped on the front door, she took a deep breath and prepared herself for a cold reception.

"I might have known she'd send you," said Kathleen as she opened the door.

Bronwyn pushed past Kathleen and immediately headed upstairs to Rosina's room.

"I'm here for her things. I won't be long," she said over her shoulder.

As she entered Rosina's room, Kathleen was right behind her.

"You can't just barge in here like this!" she said.

"I can, and I have. I'm not Rosina. I'm not frightened of you," said Bronwyn and pulled Rosie's suitcase off the top of her wardrobe. "And if you hit me, I'll hit you right back."

Kathleen gaped in shock at the nerve of the girl. How Rosina had gotten mixed up with a wild child like this one was beyond her.

But she didn't stop her from packing Rosina's things. She knew Bronwyn of old, and was aware that she didn't make empty threats. She knew Bronwyn's reputation for fighting, and she didn't want to be on the receiving end. As Bronwyn carefully and methodically packed Rosina's clothes, Kathleen backed out of the room to watch Bronwyn from the other side of Rosina's bedroom doorway. How lucky her daughter was to have this feisty girl in her life. She, Kathleen, had had nobody. Not one single soul would have been prepared to do for her what Bronwyn was doing for Rosina. Before she could start to wallow over the injustices of life, Kathleen turned on her heel and went downstairs without another word.

Bronwyn watched Kathleen leave and when she was gone she worked more quickly. With Kathleen there, she had deliberately moved at her own pace, not wanting Kathleen to think she was scared and hurrying. Now Kathleen was gone, so she moved fast, no longer folding clothes or placing them in the case in a tidy manner. It was by no means Kathleen that Bronwyn was afraid of; she knew she could handle her attacks any day – physical or verbal. No, it was the house that haunted Bronwyn more than any living person in it. Never had she known a house so cold. It was clean to the point of obsessiveness Bronwyn would have said, but that was the only part of life where Kathleen seemed to have made an effort – cleanliness. Not one ornament adorned the windowsills, no photographs, not even of Rosina. This house was a shell, nothing welcoming or homely about it. Just like the woman who owned it.

Bronwyn packed the last of Rosina's clothes, took one last look around the room, and, with a shudder, she pulled the suitcase behind her and walked back down the stairs. Kathleen waited at the bottom, standing in front of the door. Bronwyn tensed and kept right on moving until Kathleen had no choice but to move away. Bronwyn paused at the front door and turned back to face Kathleen.

"I met Connor tonight. He's a nice lad, a good lad, and it'd be a shame for you to fall out with Rosie over this."

Kathleen turned white and clenched her fists.

"Don't you give me advice on family matters!" she hissed. "Not you, with your broken home and dysfunctional mother. Don't you dare."

Bronwyn let go of the suitcase and marched back up to Kathleen.

"Why are you under the impression that my mother is dysfunctional?" she asked quietly. At the sight of the fire in Bronwyn's eyes, Kathleen shrank back against the wall.

"She is." Kathleen pulled herself up to her full height and looked Bronwyn square in the eye. "And your father – where's he, then?"

"My father left us, as you know. And I couldn't give a shit about that. Barry and I have done all right without him, just like Rosina will be fine without you."

With that she picked up the case and opened the door. She paused as she studied the crowd that had gathered again in the street to watch the James's ongoing soap opera and she turned back to Kathleen once more.

"It must feel lousy, Mrs J."

"What?" Kathleen frowned.

Bronwyn smirked and started to walk down the path.

"Losing your only child," she called over her shoulder.

Kathleen kicked the door shut and slumped in a heap on the floor. It was several minutes later before she stopped shaking enough to haul herself up. Clutching the wall for support, she went over to the mirror hanging in the hall and stared at her reflection.

They all thought that she was a cold-hearted bitch. Her neighbours, Bronwyn, even her own daughter. Well, they were right. It was the only way she had been able to survive. So deeply ingrained was this instinct, it had totally taken over every other human emotion.

* * * *

Belfast – 1960.

Kathleen was going on her first date. Well, it was a double date actually, with her best friend Susan. They were both sixteen and, after a lot of cajoling and pleading, both sets of parents had agreed to the date. They had, of course, insisted on meeting the boys in question and, when finally they were satisfied that the lads had nothing untoward in mind, they let the girls go.

Kathleen was nervous as she fixed her hair in front of her bedroom mirror, her mother sitting on the bed behind her issuing instructions.

Finally, Kathleen turned around.

"Mam, it's just the cinema. The picture finishes at nine, and I'll be home by half past. Now, how do I look?'

Glenda Morris appraised her daughter and smiled.

"Perfect," she replied.

Satisfied, Kathleen picked up her bag and took one more look in the mirror. She *did* look okay; smart black trousers and a black satin shirt, nothing that would give out the wrong impression to Marty.

"And this Marty, you like him?" asked Glenda casually.

Kathleen grinned and Glenda saw the look of puppy love in her daughter's eyes.

"He's okay," she said and kissed her mother on the cheek. "Bye!"

Glenda followed Kathleen down and sat on the bottom step as Kathleen called out to her father, Mick, who was reading the newspaper.

A car horn sounded outside and Glenda suddenly looked horrified.

"He's driving?" she asked. "How old *is* he?"

Kathleen laughed and the young and carefree sound tugged at Glenda's heart.

"It's a taxi, mam, he's in a taxi!"

Glenda nodded and was about to repeat all of her earlier warnings when Mick came out into the hall.

"Quiet, you." he directed at Glenda. "Let the poor girl go."

"Thanks, Dad." Kathleen opened the door and closed it softly behind her.

"Have a good time!" Glenda called out, but the door was already shut.

And they did have a good time. The picture was not up to their expectations so, halfway through, the foursome held a muttered conversation and decided to leave. By eight o'clock, they found themselves in the diner across the road from the cinema, frequented by the high school kids. They ordered coffees and chatted about the film, school, and what they had all done over the weekend.

Marty held Kathleen's hand under the table, and she wondered nervously if he would kiss her at the end of the night.

Later, much later, she looked at her watch and was aghast to find that it was ten o'clock. Her parents would be furious! She stood up and grabbed her coat.

"I've got to go!" she said. "I didn't realise it was so late!"

Marty stood up and reached for his coat.

"I'll walk you to the taxi rank," he said and, after a moment's consideration, she nodded her consent.

Two streets away they stood at the empty taxi rank, Kathleen wringing her hands in despair.

"Calm down," said Marty. "Look, here's one now."

Relief flooded through her and she raised her hand to signal the taxi to stop. When it drew up alongside of them, she turned to Marty.

"Thanks for tonight. Sorry I have to rush off."

He leaned in and kissed her, so fast that she barely realised it had happened. As he pulled back, she saw him blush and she squeezed his hand before jumping in the taxi.

"Manchester Road, please," she said and, as the cab pulled away, she turned to wave to Marty.

When he was out of sight, she pulled out her purse to have the cab fare ready. When she opened it, though, she was mortified to discover she didn't have enough by half to get home.

"Driver, could you just take me as far as Station Road please," she said, inwardly cursing herself for spending so much that she had left herself short. Now she would be even later in getting home, and her parents would be frantic.

Ten minutes later she was standing alone on the corner of Station road in Belfast town centre. She shivered as she pulled her coat tighter around her. She was in Protestant territory now, and she hoped to God she wouldn't run into any trouble as she made her way home.

Well, you won't get home just standing here.

So Kathleen put her head down and started the fifteen-minute walk home. She was almost onto home ground when she heard someone walking behind her. She cast a glance over her shoulder and nervous laughter bubbled up as all she saw was an old man walking his dog. She watched the old man turn down a side street and turned to walk on again.

Wham!

Kathleen was knocked off her feet. For a second she lay looking up at the night sky, not knowing what had hit her.

Then a face came into her vision, and Kathleen stared into a pair of ice blue eyes, so blue and so cold they looked dead. She opened her mouth to scream, but the man clamped his hand over her mouth so tightly it cut off all sound.

Still keeping his hand over her face, he moved around behind her and dragged her back into an alleyway.

Kathleen was petrified. He was a Protestant. He must know she was Catholic. He was going to hurt her! Shoot her!

Then he was in front of her again, and she yelped as he kneeled down on her chest, both of his legs pinning her arms to her side. She looked at his hands, trying to see the gun he would surely use but she saw nothing. He grinned suddenly. As he leaned back and his hands went to the zipper on his trousers, her blood ran cold.

Survival instinct took over and she thrashed around beneath him, desperate, willing to take a bullet or a knife if it meant he didn't do *that* to her.

For a second he looked surprised at her sudden attempt to get free, before he gained control again by grasping her hair and banging her head hard on the concrete. She lay dazed. As her head thumped with pain, she knew that this was a fight she had lost. Sensing her inability to struggle anymore, he worked quickly. He tore off the new black trousers that weren't supposed to give anyone the wrong impression, and threw them carelessly to one side. It didn't last long, but the pain was intense and she turned her head to one side, stuffing her fist in her own mouth to stop herself screaming, lest he hurt her even more.

Towards the end, she drifted away, near to unconsciousness, and it seemed like a lifetime later when she realised that he had gone.

"Oh, my God...Jesus Lord Christ, help me..." she muttered as she struggled to sit up.

The pain in her head intensified, and she slumped back to the ground.

"Help me…please…" she cried.

But nobody answered her plea.

How Kathleen got home in the state that she was in, she didn't know. When it became clear that nobody would come to her aid, she grabbed her discarded clothing and staggered off down the street. When Kathleen finally reached home, she started to weep as she saw her mother standing on the front step.

Glenda, anxious as she glanced at her watch, caught sight of Kathleen staggering up the road. She blanched as she took stock of her daughter with her bloodied, tear streaked face, clutching her trousers in her hand.

"Mick!" She screamed and ran up the road to meet Kathleen.

She stopped a few feet short of Kathleen and knew immediately what had happened. It was every mother's worst nightmare; that your boy goes out for the evening and ends up kneecapped or your girl comes home raped. Murders, general muggings, car accidents – these all happened, but, for some reason, the scenario that occurs to every mother that frets when her daughter is late is always this one. And now, for Glenda, it had all come horrifyingly true.

Glenda reached out, wanting desperately to gather Kathleen up in her arms and comfort her like she had when she was a little girl and had fallen off her bike, but something stopped her. Maybe it was the sight of Kathleen's chubby, white thighs streaked with blood and shiny, silver mucus, or the mass of grass and twigs that clung to Kathleen's hair.

"Mammy?" Kathleen whispered in a small voice and Glenda snapped out of it, realising she had been staring at her daughter with an almost morbid curiosity.

Suddenly, Mick was there. With one look he also knew, and with an order for Glenda to call the police, he scooped Kathleen up in his arms and took her into the house.

The rest of the night was a blur of action. Police statements, examinations and questions, and then a dash to the hospital to have five stitches in the back of her head.

"Was it Marty?" Glenda asked at one point and Kathleen shook her head fiercely.

Dear Marty, he won't want me now.

In those days, rape was an uncomfortable subject to discuss and the three of them dealt with it in their own way. Glenda was weepy, Mick refused to discuss it, and Kathleen blacked it out completely.

In fact, she avoided thinking about the event so successfully that when she discovered she was pregnant, for a moment it confused her totally.

How can I be pregnant? I'm sixteen years old and I don't have a boyfriend. I'm still a virgin!

But pregnant she was and, as a Catholic, abortion was totally out of the question.

"You'll have to marry the father," said Glenda in a moment of madness.

Kathleen stared at her mother with undisguised shock.

"Mam, the father *raped* me! I don't know where he lives! I don't even know his name!"

Glenda flinched at the word *rape*, and while the broken family tried to come up with a solution, life went on.

It was early into Kathleen's third month of the pregnancy, as she was taking a hot bath, when Glenda came into the bathroom and closed the door quietly behind her.

"I brought you a drink," said Glenda and set a tray down on the floor.

Kathleen, who had been dozing, opened her eyes and looked down at the tray. Her eyes bulged at the tray's contents and she raised her eyes to meet her mother's.

Glenda refused to look at her daughter. Instead, she stood up and as quietly as she had entered she left the room.

Kathleen clutched the side of the bath and looked again at the tray.

There were only two items on it – a full bottle of gin, and a wire coat hanger.

She lay back in the hot water and tentatively touched her stomach. It was still flat, no sign of life yet, but she knew it was there.

How she hated it.

How she instinctively loved it.

Two such powerful emotions and both at the same time, directed at the same thing, were totally overwhelming.

She glanced back at the tray and picked up the bottle of gin. Before she could lose her nerve, she flipped off the lid and watched as it bounced across the bathroom floor. Then she held the bottle to her lips and took a long swig. It was her first taste of gin and she nearly vomited then and there. But she swallowed and took a second gulp of the foul liquor.

Over the next thirty minutes or so she managed to down a quarter of the bottle. Her stomach began to churn. She put the bottle aside and picked up the coat hanger. Concentrating on unwinding the hanger so it became a neat strip of wire, she tried not to think about what she had to with the thing once she had finished. Soon it was straight, and Kathleen lay back again and stretched her legs out in front of her.

I can't do this!

She hurled the coat hanger across the room and it landed near the door, next to the gin bottle lid.

Maybe the gin will work on its own.

She topped up the bath water from the hot tap and retrieved the bottle of gin once more.

After a couple more swigs, she studied the bottle of gin intently.

What am I doing? This baby is not its father. It's half of me, a part of me.

Reaching over, she poured the rest of the bottle into the sink.

When she came downstairs in her dressing gown, she sat opposite Mick and Glenda on the couch.

"I think I should go away for a while," she said.

That was how Kathleen came to travel eighty miles south of Belfast, to a small town called Crossmaglen. When she decided she was keeping the baby, her parents began to make arrangements. Her name was changed to Kathleen James and Mick sorted out the house on Willoughby Street. It was frightening, but liberating at the same time. For the last part of the pregnancy Kathleen was able to convince herself that this baby was wanted. The story for the neighbours was easy. Kathleen was a child bride who was now a young widow. They bought the story and, due to her aloofness, they mostly left her alone.

The labour, when it happened, was mercifully quick. So fast, in fact, that when the midwife arrived, Kathleen had already done most of the work.

Later, when she had been cleaned up and was resting in her bed, the midwife handed the baby to her.

Kathleen waited until the woman had left the room before she looked down at her child.

"Rosina," she murmured, and pulled aside the shawl that the baby girl was wrapped in.

She waited for a moment for the lightning bolt of love for her child to hit her. When it didn't, she turned her head and, through her tears, stared out of the window.

I hate my baby. Dear God, I hate her.

Things didn't get better. While the baby had been in her womb, Kathleen had wanted it, or at least convinced herself that she did. But now that it was out and in her arms, the child just served as a reminder of what had happened.

Kathleen waited patiently for her parents to visit her. Her mother would know what to do; she would be able to teach her how to stop the baby crying, show her the right way to bathe her.

Her parents never arrived.

That was the way it was to be. Kathleen and Rosina, on their own, in Crossmaglen for the foreseeable future.

When Rosina started school, she questioned Kathleen about her father. Kathleen told her what she had told the neighbours; her father was dead.

The maternal feelings never came. Rosina grew up and never wanted for anything. Anything that is, except the most important thing – a mother's love.

That was Kathleen's story.

After more than twenty years of misery raising Rosina, the girl had done her the biggest disservice by running off with a Protestant.

As Kathleen stared at herself in the mirror, she felt emptiness so deep in her soul that life barely seemed worth living.

Chapter Seven

A Fresh Start

When Mary and Rosina returned home later that night, Bronwyn was waiting on the front steps with Rosina's suitcase.

She stood up when they came through the front gate, and gestured to the case.

"Piece of cake," she said.

Rosina shook her head in wonder and wished that she could handle her mother the way Bronwyn could.

"Are you coming in?" she asked and turned to Mary. "If that's okay?"

Mary nodded and opened the door.

"You have to treat this as your home now," she said, and disappeared into the lounge. "Kettle's in the kitchen, stick it on for us."

Bronwyn tugged at Rosina's sleeve as they made their way up the hall to the kitchen.

"What's she like?" asked Bronwyn in a stage whisper.

"Nice," Rosina whispered back. "She was like ice when I first met her, but we talked and she's on our side. I think she could be just as scary as my mother, though!"

"Don't worry about Kathleen anymore. You've got us now," said Bronwyn. "Don't let the bastards get you down."

Rosina thought briefly of her mother as she filled the kettle with water.

No, she wouldn't think about her. Kathleen had done nothing in her life to support her.

As much as it saddened her, she would just have to forget that she ever had a mother.

* * * *

The 17th December dawned as a perfect winter morning, crisp and bright, with a layer of frost on the cars, and the promise of early snow in the air.

Rosina awoke early, and for a moment couldn't figure out where she was. With a jolt, it all came back to her and she felt a simmer of excitement as she realised she was in Connor's house.

What would the arrangements be when Connor came home from the hospital? Rosina couldn't very well see Mary allowing them both to stay in the same room, let alone the same bed. Never mind, being in the same house was satisfaction enough for her.

She hopped out of bed and pulled open the window. The view was not much different from her bedroom window; row upon row of terrace houses and miles of cobbled streets. Streets that she knew so well already from her sneaking around here in the last six months. She heard the faint sound of a radio coming from the kitchen. She was about to close the window and venture downstairs, when the window below her opened and she saw Mary stick her head out.

Mary glanced left and right before lighting up a cigarette. The smoke drifted slowly up to Rosina's window.

"Hi," she called.

Mary looked up and spotted Rosina.

"Oh, morning." Mary glanced at the cigarette in her hand. "I'm supposed to have quit."

"Well, given all that's happened, I think one will be okay." Rosina tried but failed to keep the amusement out of her voice.

Mary turned back to stare out in front of her.

"My lungs, anyways," Rosina heard her mutter.

Giggling quietly, Rosina pulled back into the room and closed the window against the cold morning air. Slipping on her dressing gown, she ran down the stairs and into the lounge.

Mary had now retreated into the room and stood with her cigarette held out of the window.

"Sleep well?"

"Like a log," Rosina affirmed. "Can I get you some tea?"

"Nope." Mary flicked the cigarette out and watched it land on the lawn. "We're going out for breakfast. My treat."

Rosina paused and wrapped her gown tighter around her.

"Is that a good idea?" she asked. "I mean, people will know who I am."

Mary closed the window and turned to face Rosina, a look of determination on her face.

"I don't care. I'm not going to let history repeat itself. It's not going to happen again, not to my boy."

With that, she marched out of the room. "Get dressed," Rosina heard her say as she climbed the stairs.

With a feeling of trepidation, Rosina did as she was told.

* * * *

Bronwyn's start to the day was not as pleasant. She too awoke early. Too early, she thought as she glanced at the luminous dial of her clock. It was only six o'clock. She sat up and realised that Danny had woken her.

"Are you coming or going?" she asked coldly.

Danny pulled the duvet over him.

"Coming," was his muffled reply.

"Fuck," she whispered and pulled back the quilt.

"Hey!" He clutched it back, but she was quick and pulled it right off the bed.

"This isn't fair, Dan. You come and go when you please, and this isn't even your house!"

"Oh, Jesus." Danny sat up and swung his legs over the side of the bed. "What do you want from me, Bronwyn?"

Bronwyn paused and took a moment to think.

What did she want? For Danny to stop with his nocturnal missions for one, for him to stop with his belief that all Protestants were evil and that all Brits should be shot. Suddenly a thought struck her, and she smiled.

"Let's not fight," she said. "I'm sorry."

Danny raised his eyebrows and said nothing.

She pulled the quilt back across the room and put it on the bed.

"You get some sleep. Sleep in as late as you want. And then, this afternoon we're going to spend some time together."

Danny took back the duvet and wrapped it around him. He was obviously suspicious, as he knew how Bronwyn's mind worked, but he said nothing.

Quickly and quietly, Bronwyn dressed and picked up her bag. She cast a look at the sleeping man in her bed and smiled. She knew how to make everything all right again. She would take Danny to meet Connor. Connor need never know that Danny had anything to do with the shooting, and Danny would be able to see that not all Protestants were worthless.

* * * *

Stu Jackson's day never really began. It didn't begin because the day before had never ended. They had driven through the night across England, boarded the ferry at Galloway, and crossed the sea into Bangor. Sleep was impossible on the rough sea crossing, and Stu left the Land Rover to stand on the deck as they approached Ireland. Dawn broke as they docked, and he returned to the vehicle as they lined up to leave the ferry.

He glanced at Tommy and Sam, who were both sleeping soundly, and pulled out the letters that he had written to Ellie during the journey. His first priority was to post them as soon as possible. Then he would search for a phone to call and let her know he had arrived safely.

Stu must have nodded off, because the next thing he knew, they were all woken by the vehicle stopping sharply. Stu hauled himself up and peered through the front windscreen.

"Christ, is this it?" he asked, and the corporal who was driving nodded.

Tommy shoved Stu aside and looked out of the window.

The land surrounding the fields was shrouded in a thin mist. The trees were bare and the fields were also empty – no animals, no crops, the earth itself looked like some sort of rocky terrain that wouldn't grow anything, even if someone were to try. The land looked like it had been stripped.

"Looks like a shit heap to me," he commented. "Are we gonna sit here all day?"

"Gotta get clearance to take the car through. Security is high here and you've been put on full scale alert."

"Alert for what?" asked Stu.

The driver glanced back at Steve.

"This is Northern Ireland. What do *you* reckon?"

Stu shut up and sat back while the driver spoke to the guy in the little security hut. Eventually the iron gates were opened, and the car moved into the camp.

Before the Land Rover had parked, somebody was banging on the rear doors and they were yanked open. Another corporal stood there and he regarded the three in the back.

"Come on out, lads, can't hang around. You're like sitting ducks here."

Stu jumped out of the car and looked around. His fears were recognised; the scene before his eyes was dismal. The camp was small, maybe a hundred square metres. Four wooden buildings lined the six-foot fence, which was topped with barbed wire. In opposite corners of the camp stood two observation towers, the third Sanger in another corner. There was a landing pad for the helicopters that made daily stops with supplies and post, and not much else.

Stu looked back and realised that the others had disappeared. He caught a glimpse of Tommy heading into one of the buildings. The corporal stuck his head out of the door and beckoned Stu over.

"This is your barracks," he said. "That one is where you eat, that one is where you shit."

With all four buildings accounted for, Stu nodded and felt his heart sink as he went into his sleeping area.

It was like a concentration camp. Bunk beds lined the walls. The soldiers currently in residence had tried to personalise their sleeping spaces with photographs and posters, but it didn't disguise the depressing place that would be his home this Christmas.

With a sigh, he slung his bag on the bed and sloped off to find a phone.

* * * *

Rosina walked alongside Mary with her head down. She had been right to be nervous; Mary's neighbours were out in force as news of Rosina's arrival in the Dean household spread along the grapevine. However, when they saw her with Mary they did nothing more than stare.

"I guess you really are respected," muttered Rosina as they walked briskly along.

"Damn right I am. They know what they'll get from me if they say anything," replied Mary.

Eventually, Mary stopped outside the Cross Coffee House and opened the door.

All eyes looked up as Mary ushered Rosina into a booth near the window. Rosina glanced around and blushed as she saw all of the staff and customers staring at her.

A waitress came over and, without a word, slammed two menus on the table.

The waitress turned and started to walk away. As she passed Rosina, she spoke quietly without breaking stride.

"I should throw you out of here."

Rosina said nothing, but Mary noted that her eyes filled with tears.

Once the waitress had returned to the kitchen, Mary pulled a crumpled pack of cigarettes out of her pocket and lit one up.

"You're gonna have to toughen up, girl."

"It's hard. I never did anything to these people," said Rosina.

"But your father did, and his father before him. This is a war that's been going on for years, and it won't stop for a while yet. If you're serious about Connor, you're going to have to learn to live with it, or stick up for yourself," replied Mary.

"I am serious about Connor. I love him," said Rosina.

"And what about your parents? You're going to have to speak with them sooner or later," said Mary.

"I won't speak to my mam again. And my dad's dead."

Mary frowned as she studied the menu.

"How did he die?"

Rosina shrugged and it suddenly struck her as odd that she didn't know the details of her father's death.

"I don't know. Mam never spoke about him, except to tell me that he was dead." Suddenly, she was embarrassed. "Doesn't it sound silly? Mary…I don't know anything about him."

Mary frowned.

"Who was he? What was his name?"

Rosina shrugged.

"I don't know. I asked mam about him once, when I was old enough to realise the other kids all had a father, even if they weren't around."

"And what did she say?" Mary was intrigued now.

"She got mad—really angry." Rosina reddened and looked down at the table top. "She hit me."

Mary shook her head and bit back the barrage of abuse that she wanted to spit out about Rosina's mother.

"Okay, well…" Unable to find any words of comfort, Mary settled for patting Rosina's hand. "You're with us now, okay? Order what you want and then we'll go up to the hospital. See if we can't get Connor out of that place."

Rosina brightened at the prospect of having Connor back again. As she opened the menu and studied it, she forgot for a while that she was currently the most hated girl this side of Crossmaglen.

* * * *

When Danny heard Bronwyn leave the house, he jumped out of bed. He opened her wardrobe and pulled out the bag he had stashed there upon his return in the early hours. Pulling on his clothes, he made his way downstairs, hoping that the rest of the house was empty.

It wasn't.

Barry sat in the kitchen, nursing a steaming cup of tea and staring into space. He started when he saw Danny.

"Hey, Dan. Didn't realise you were here."

"Just on my way out actually," Danny said uneasily.

"Oh, well, don't let me stop you. Catch you later, yeah?" Barry picked up his tea and went upstairs.

Danny waited for a moment until he was sure Barry had gone. When he was satisfied, he left quietly by the back door.

Barry stood on the landing and, pulling back the curtain, peered out of the window. He waited for a while after he had heard the door close, but saw no sign of Danny leaving the house. A thought struck him and he hurried across the landing and into Bronwyn's room. Looking out of the window, he was just in time to see Danny disappear into the shed at the end of the garden.

"Jesus," whispered Barry to himself.

Danny must be using their deserted shed as a place to stash his weapons, arms and *God knows what else* for the I.R.A.

He moved back and sat on Bronwyn's bed. This was something he should report straight to Johnny, but this was *Danny*.

The guy he thought of as his brother.

In the shed that had not been used since Barry's father had left them, Danny was hard at work. He cleared a space on the worktable and pulled the supplies out of his bag that Andy, his cell leader, had given him. Along with these, he pulled out a sack of fertiliser and set about making a batch of mixed bombs. He made six of these and packed them carefully back in the bag. Next, he turned his attention to his own personal favourite; the blast bomb. This particular explosive was derived from a mixture of weed killer and sugar. A simple, but deadly, mixture that he packed tightly and carefully into empty beer cans.

His job done, he wiped off his hands and looked around the shed. Spotting a half-full box of nails, he couldn't resist making two hefty nail bombs for the forthcoming attack that he had discussed with the cell the night before.

Finally finished, he hid the bag containing the explosives underneath the table and left the shed.

Minutes later, Barry came into the shed and looked around. Danny had left empty-handed. Whatever he had done was still here. There was not much to search; the cupboards were empty, tabletop clear. He looked under the bench and carefully pulled out the bag that Danny had held when Barry had seen him in the kitchen. He opened it and cautiously pulled out the beer cans and the packages. From his time undercover in the I.R.A, he knew immediately what it all was. Mixed Bombs, blast bombs and nail bombs. It could only spell one thing; Danny's cell was organising a horrific attack, and it was up to Barry to stop it.

But, that would mean grassing on Danny.

Barry sank to the floor as he realised that he had a terrible choice to make.

* * * *

"Connor will be able to go home tomorrow," said the nurse, and Mary and Rosina exchanged glances of relief.

"Can we see him now?" asked Mary.

"Of course."

As they were about to enter Connor's room, Rosina heard her name being called. She turned to see Bronwyn dashing down the hall.

"Hey, Bronwyn," said Rosina, delighted to see her friend.

"How is he?" Bronwyn stooped over to catch her breath.

"He'll be home tomorrow," replied Rosina. "We're just about to go and see him."

"Why don't you two go in? I can come back later," said Mary.

"Are you sure?" asked Rosina.

"Of course. He'll have enough of me clucking over him when he gets home!" said Mary.

"Thanks, Missus D," said Bronwyn.

Connor was sitting up in bed looking quite bored when they went in. His eyes lit up when he saw the two girls.

"You look much better," said Rosina and pulled a chair up to his bed. "Have you been told about going home?"

"Yeah, can't wait. And it'll be so great with you being there," replied Connor. "Hi, Bronwyn."

"Hi. Do you reckon you'll be up for a trip to the pub tomorrow?" asked Bronwyn.

"Well, they've given me those," Connor gestured to a pair of crutches. "I'm sure I could stagger down to the pub."

"Is that a good idea?" Rosina asked anxiously. "Mary took me to breakfast this morning and you should have seen the looks and comments I got."

"Fuck 'em!" retorted Bronwyn. "I'm bringing Danny, and once they see you two with him and me, nobody will touch you."

"Danny!" Rosina exclaimed. "We all know how he feels about, well, people like Connor."

"Who's Danny?" Connor looked confused.

"He's my guy. And he'll do whatever I tell him to, so don't you two worry," Bronwyn stood up and blew a kiss. "Tomorrow, we'll be at your place early evening."

Bronwyn took the bus home and, on a whim, she got off three stops early and stood at the Divide.

It was not a physical divide. No fence, hedge, or visible border distinguished it from one part of town to the other, but all of the residents knew exactly where it was. Nobody crossed it, unless it was Republicans crossing to make trouble like they had for Connor the other night. Even kids no longer dared each other to cross the Divide.

Years ago, her mother had told her, Republicans and Loyalists had lived all over the town, side by side. When the troubles turned ferocious around 1969, the council had moved the Protestants to council houses on the other side of town. That was when the Divide was born. Bronwyn couldn't fathom the complexities of the war that ravaged her home country. It was just two religions, two sets of beliefs, two different chains of thought on whether this country should be joined with another. Why couldn't people agree to disagree?

She took two steps and found herself in Protestant territory.

It was strange; she shivered, feeling suddenly naked and vulnerable. She moved back over to her side and stood there for a while longer, looking around. Eventually, she pulled her scarf tighter around her and started to walk home.

* * * *

"What do you think about Protestants, Ma?"

It was early evening and Bronwyn found herself alone with her mother.

Alia stopped stirring the Irish stew and looked over at Bronwyn.

"I was friends with a Prod once," she said, a faraway look in her eyes.

Bronwyn sat up straighter.

"Tell me," she demanded.

Alia turned the temperature on the stove down and came to sit with her daughter.

"It was such a big part of my life, yet I never told anyone. Not even your dad."

"Tell me," Bronwyn repeated.

Alia sighed, and began her story.

Chapter Eight

Alia

Crossmaglen 1952.

"It was hard work for my mam. There were ten of us, you see, and it wasn't so bad during the school term, but the holidays were a nightmare for her. Da worked the mines all day, literally from dawn 'til dusk, so ten of us running around the house was a handful. So every summer holiday us kiddies would be split up. Some of would go to Belfast to me Nan's and the rest would go to me Auntie's in Portadown. We didn't mind at all, it was our summer holiday and it gave me mam a break so everyone was happy. I always went to Belfast with my three brothers, the twins, who were sixteen and your Uncle Ryan, who was eighteen that first year I went. Of course, they didn't want their kid sister hanging around and after the first endless week baking everyday with Nan I got bored. So, the next week I went out on my own, and I felt so grown up, not being allowed out far on my own at home. That was when I met Cally.

"I went down to Lake Neagh and it was beautiful; it seemed like the ocean to me. There were even sandy shores all the way around it, and because it didn't lead into the sea there were no oil slicks or anything to spoil the beauty of the water. I sat there for a while, and it was the first time in my life that I'd ever known peace and quiet. After a while, I realised that I wasn't alone, there was another girl there. She was on the opposite side of the lake and I looked around for her parents,

71

but she was alone too. I waved, hesitantly like, and she gave a sort of half wave back. I wanted desperately to talk to her. I hadn't thought that there were any other ten-year-old girls in Belfast but, like kiddies that age, I didn't dare. Stupidly, we both sat on our own sides of the lake until the sun began to set and I skipped back to Nan's.

"The next day I got up early and returned to the lake. She was already there, and this time I'd come prepared. I approached her and offered her some of the bread I'd nicked from Nan's house. She took some and we sat there eating the dry crusts until we'd finished the bag. Then she pulled out some mints from her pocket and we shared those, too. Her name was Cally, she told me, Cally Wilson and she was the same age as me. We traded stories that day and arranged to meet up again every day for the rest of my time there.

"Cally was very pretty, total opposite to me. She was all petite and blonde, the sort of girl you know is going to be a right show stopper when she hit her teenage years.

"And she was, for I saw Cally Wilson every single summer holiday for the next nine years. Except for one, when I was made to go to Portadown to me Auntie's, and by God, I kicked up such a fuss they never made me go there again.

"Of course, we knew we were different from each other in a very important way as we grew up, but we didn't really understand it. And by the time we did understand what it was all about, we had a bond that was too deep to break. We had grown up, grown out of Barbie dolls and into Ken dolls, if you know what I mean. We still spent most summer days down by the lake, though. It was our special place. Nobody bothered us there, not like they did when we went into the town. By that time I had been going there every summer, so all the Prods knew about us. Cally lost a few friends by sticking with me, and I made myself a few enemies, but as long as we had each other we could deal with it.

"Then, it all ended as suddenly as it began."

Bronwyn sat transfixed and she tugged impatiently on her mother's arm when she stopped talking.

"What happened, Ma?" Bronwyn asked.

Alia looked up and straight into the eyes of her only daughter. She took a moment to study her child before she continued with her story.

"We'd been at the lake all day. We no longer went into town, or to the discos. Things had changed – no longer were we just getting called names, things had started to get violent. It was a good day, but it was long past nightfall so I walked Cally to her house. I always made sure she got home first. She was smaller than me and not so tough. Rosina reminds me a lot of Cally, you know. Anyhow, we knew that something was wrong before we even got near to her house. The air was thick with black, acrid smoke and crowds of people were running down the street.

"Cally stopped and clutched at my arm. I looked over at her and I could read her mind, her prayer, before she spoke the words.

"'Not my house.'

"We broke into a run and pushed through the people to get to the front of the crowd. It *was* her house. Of course it was – we had known in the pits of our stomachs it would be her house.

"Cally stood outside her own garden gate and stared in horror at her burning home.

"'Where are the fire engines?' I remember calling. 'Someone, call them, please!'

"Suddenly, a movement caught our eye in the upstairs window and Cally let out a shriek as she realised that it was her mother.

"I'd never met her mam, none of her family in fact. Not because they didn't approve of me. They let Cally go her own way in seeing me. It was just easier to see Cally on our own. That was why we stopped going to the bars and the town centre.

"Now, I felt my heart rip for what Cally was seeing, a sight so terrible it still burns my eyelids every time I close my eyes. Cally's mam was on fire, her back, arms and hair, yet she was frantically trying to open the window. I stared at her and all the while Cally shrieked beside me, sounding like a little Jay bird, shrieking and shrieking. Then the heat blew the window in and suddenly her mam was there, leaning out as far as she could and I saw the baby that she held in her arms. I saw what she was going to do and I knew, without looking, that Cally would not be able to move. Nobody else was helping and it was up to me. I crashed through the gate and stood directly under the window, just as she let the baby go. That was the longest moment of my life as I stood there and watched that babe fall. I knew I had to catch it, there was no second chance and if I missed, that child would die at my feet on the concrete."

Alia stopped speaking and clapped a hand to her eyes as though to stop herself reliving the memory.

"Mam? Mam!" Bronwyn bought Alia out of her reverie and she snapped her head up.

Bronwyn was horrified to see the tears slide down Alia's cheeks. She couldn't remember ever seeing her mother cry before.

"Did you catch the baby?" Bronwyn was wide eyed, hoping, praying for the baby she didn't even know.

More tears slid out of Alia's eyes and she reached across the table and gripped Bronwyn's hand.

"Mam? Did you catch it?"

There was a long silence, and then, "No."

Bronwyn swallowed the lump that had risen in her throat and gaped at her mother.

"No?"

Alia took a deep breath and swiped at her eyes.

"I was standing there, watching the babe fall and it was fine, he was right on track, then the downstairs window blew and I was literally picked up and thrown right back out of the garden and into the road by the force of the blast. So, no, I didn't catch him." Alia looked back up and tried to smile. "He was a little boy, just six months old. Shane was his name."

"Oh, Ma." Bronwyn wished she had never coerced her mother into telling her this story.

"And that was that. I never saw Cally again. Her whole family had been wiped out by that damn fire, and when they discovered it had been deliberately started, most likely by one of the thugs who had a grudge against the open-minded family, Cally moved away."

"I'm sorry," said Bronwyn. "But, why didn't you see Cally again?"

"It was indirectly my fault, don't you see?" Alia stood up and returned to the stew on the stove. "I'd caused trouble in their lives. Oh, I know it wasn't all me. I found out since that Cally's mam had her own Catholic friends, but she kept that well hidden. Just not hidden enough."

Bronwyn looked down at the table, feeling like her heart would burst.

"I can't stand it, Ma!" she exclaimed suddenly. "I don't understand this hatred at all."

Alia laughed and the humourless sound pierced Bronwyn.

"Get used to it, sweetheart. Stick around here and it's something you'll live with forever."

"No, I won't. I won't put up with it. You'll see. I can change people, make them see the fighting is worthless," Bronwyn's voice was cold and hard enough to make Alia turn and come back to the table.

"My girl, where did you get your spirit from?" Alia smiled and shook her head in wonder. "But, Bronwyn, if anybody can, you can."

It was all that she needed to hear. As she kissed her mother and left the room, she had a newfound resolve to unite Danny and Connor.

It was only two people, sure, but it would be a start.

* * * *

Barry woke suddenly and turned over to look at the clock. 4:45 a.m.

Damnit, he was waking earlier and earlier each day; yesterday he had at least slept until 5:00a.m.

The sleeping problem had not gone away since it first began three weeks ago. Barry had paid a visit to the local library and spent an afternoon perusing the books on his now specialist subject.

Insomnia.

From the books that he had devoured, he had discovered that the form of insomnia he was suffering from was premature waking. He had also discovered that there were many remedies that were recommended, ranging from honeycomb to warm milk, before getting onto the heavy-duty stuff that would require a trip to the doctor. The doctor was something he wanted to avoid; both the I.R.A and the British government had access to medical records, and he could get pulled from both teams if they suspected his mind was not entirely on the job. Of course, this was highly illegal of both parties, but then both groups involved didn't always play by the rulebook.

Barry lay in his bed for a while longer before he got up and flicked the lamp on. It was depressing, this *illness*, and he didn't know how much longer he could put up with it. He wished he could talk to Bronwyn about it, about everything, but she was asleep with Danny, and what could she do anyway?

He turned his mind to a more pressing matter. He had a meeting with Johnny in six hours. He knew he should tell Johnny about the mass of explosives that were currently residing in his garden shed, but if he did Danny would be arrested by the Royal Ulster Constabulary and it would be over for him for a very long time.

What about Bronwyn? Could he stand to put her through the pain, knowing that he had caused it?

"I want out—just want out of this whole mess," he muttered to himself.

Suddenly he stopped pacing, and it was as if a light bulb had gone on in his head.

That was it! He would get out of the whole rat race; leave the I.R.A, quit the agent role—that was all he needed to do.

They won't leave you alone, either of them, the annoying little voice in his head said.

"Then I'll leave Crossmaglen. I can make a fresh start someplace else and leave all this sorry shit behind me."

Pushing from his mind thoughts of Bronwyn and his mother, Barry lay back on the bed feeling like a little bit of pressure had been released from his increasingly tortured self.

As soon as the sun started to rise in the east, Barry got dressed and paid a visit to Johnny. He didn't go to Johnny's house; he didn't even know where the man lived. He called him from the telephone box at the end of the road and told Johnny he needed to see him, urgently. Johnny, sounding like he had been asleep, named a café that they had met in a couple of times. Barry hung up and started to walk.

Johnny was already seated to the rear of the café when Barry arrived. He slid into the seat opposite him.

"Coffee?" asked Johnny.

"No, nothing for me," replied Barry and took a deep breath. "I want to quit my job."

Johnny regarded him with some amusement before he spoke.

"The agent job or the I.R.A one?" he asked.

"The agent…I mean, both," said Barry, wondering why Johnny always made him so nervous.

"That's a sudden decision to make. Why would you want to do that?"

"I can't do it anymore. I can't betray Danny and I can't risk my sister being hurt. It's just all too much."

"It would be a shame to lose you," said Johnny.

"I can't help that."

"Well—" Johnny sat back and laced his hands behind his head. "I'll have to take this news back to my boss. We'll get back to you."

Barry frowned.

"Why would you need to get back to me? I've quit. That's it, the end of it."

"Oh, Barry, you know it doesn't work like that. We need more meetings. We need to make sure you've not switched sides and are using information against us."

Barry suddenly felt very weary and he rubbed his head as he felt a tension headache coming on. He should have just left the country without telling anyone.

"I'm quitting the cell today," he said in reply. "You can check, use your resources, then we'll need no more meetings."

"Of course," Johnny's tone was ever so slightly patronising and Barry felt a flicker of anger as he sensed that he wasn't being taken seriously.

"Are we done?" asked Barry.

Johnny nodded and raised a hand in farewell. Barry left the café, more confused than when he had arrived.

As he walked along, he felt the hairs on the back of his neck prick up and he glanced furtively around. That man, by the Indian takeaway, was he watching him? Barry snapped his head forward and let out an audible gasp as he saw Andy, his cell leader, leaving the newsagent across the street. Good God, had Andy been following him? Did he know that he had been with Johnny, and did he know who Johnny was?

Sweat gathered on Barry's brow and he chewed his fingernails anxiously. Were both sides watching him?

Get a grip.

Trying to steady his breathing, he walked briskly on. As soon as he was out of sight of the café, he broke into a run.

* * * *

Back at the Ranger home, Barry's mother, Alia, wasn't in much better shape than her son. Her talk with Bronwyn had got her thinking about the past. More specifically, it had got her reminiscing about Cally. After an hour of mentally listing the pros and cons, Alia had decided to get in touch with her old best friend. She sat down at the kitchen table with the cordless phone and the national telephone directory. Predictably, there were a lot of Wilson's, so she started with the initial 'C' in case Cally had never married. She rang them all, seven of them in total, with no luck and decided to start back at the beginning.

It took her right through to the 'F's before she reached Francine, a lady who claimed to be Cally's aunt.

"And she'd be my age, thirty-eight, right?" Alia asked in excitement.

"That's her. Wait a second, I should have her number." Francine put the phone down and Alia heard her muttering as she flicked through her own phone book.

"Now, you have to dial the whole number. Have you got a pen?" Francine came back on the line.

"Yes, go ahead." Alia wrote down the number that Francine reeled off and frowned as she stared at it.

"It seems to have a lot of digits," she said.

She heard a chuckle from Francine's end.

"It is a lot of digits. You *are* calling New York, after all. Will you give her my love when you ring her?"

"Oh. Yes, yes, of course, and thank you for your help."

Alia hung up the phone.

New York. Who would have thought it? Well, after the death of her family there was not much point in staying in Belfast, after all.

It took another half an hour before Alia built up the courage to ring the number, and even then she hung up four times before she completed dialing.

"For God's sake, all she can do is hang up," Alia said crossly and this time she made herself dial the number in full.

It rang so many times that Alia was about to ring off when she heard a small voice at the end of the line.

"Can I speak to Cally please?" she asked, palms beginning to sweat.

"Speaking."

Alia froze and tried to speak but no words came out.

80

"Hello?" The voice on the other end, which had a slight American twang to it, bought Alia back and she cleared her throat.

"Cally, it's Alia."

There was a pause from the other end, and then, "Good God!" The American accent vanished, and Cally's lilting Irish voice brought tears to Alia's eyes. "You're the one person I didn't expect to call. It's been so long."

"I know. I was speaking to my daughter about you, and it brought back so many memories that I thought I would try to find you."

"You have a daughter!" Cally exclaimed. "How old is she?"

"She's twenty-one. I have a son too, they're twins."

"Twenty-one eh? I'm only just starting on the baby front." Cally sounded happy enough to talk, so Alia relaxed and began to ask Cally about her life over the last two decades.

They spoke for a long time, covering everything from marriages to births and the jobs that the women had done. The one thing that neither of them mentioned was the fire that had killed Cally's family.

Bronwyn came in as they ended their conversation with a promise to keep in touch. She sat down as Alia hung up the phone.

"You'll never guess who that was!" Alia said before Bronwyn could speak.

"Who?"

"Cally, my friend Cally, who I told you about. Oh, boy, it was so good to speak to her again. You'll never guess where she's living now."

Bronwyn listened as her mother recounted the conversation and felt happy that she had finally made contact with her lost friend.

"So, you see, you were right. We just have to have the courage to try to change things," her mother was saying.

At that point Barry came in and both women blanched at the sight of him.

"You okay, Barry?" asked Alia.

"What?" Barry spun around. It was as if he hadn't even seen them sitting at the table. "Oh yes, fine thanks."

With that, he turned and left the kitchen.

Alia began to talk about Cally once more, but Bronwyn's mind was now elsewhere. She knew Barry better than anyone in this world, and he hadn't looked right. At first he gave the impression that he was drunk, but that hadn't been it either. He had just looked...wrong.

Still annoyed at him for his I.R.A betrayal, Bronwyn pushed her concerns from her mind and turned her attention back to her mother.

Chapter Nine

The Decline of Crossmaglen

Stu awoke with a start and sat bolt upright in his bunk. He wondered what had woken him and then realised that it was the alarm on his watch. He groaned as he realised it was just after midnight, and he was due on duty. Already running late, he grabbed his ration of tea bags, writing paper, and some chocolate, and ran over to the observation tower. The man who had been on duty since four o'clock yesterday afternoon was waiting impatiently. Stu apologised as he climbed up and signed in.

Stu, no stranger to the midnight patrol, had a love-hate relationship with all of the observation towers he had frequented in his army life. An eight hour shift, totally alone up a tower, would drive anyone into a depression, but Stu also welcomed the time alone with his thoughts, when he could write letters home and sometimes use the telephone, if there was more than one line.

The soldier coming off duty ran Stu through the ropes. When he was satisfied that Stu had all of the code words and knew the drill in the case of any unwanted visitors in the barracks, he made his way down the tower and Stu watched him disappear into the little wooden building.

He stood up and looked around the little room. It was circular in shape, maybe sixteen feet in diameter. It was all glass, bullet proof of course, and on a clear night one could see for miles in every direction. Along half of the room was a series of computer screens. These were set up on an infrared frequency to detect any human movement in the camp from the body heat that was radiated. He saw a red shape moving now on one of the screens and he followed it as it moved across the camp. Grabbing his binoculars, he worked out from the computer where the intruder was supposed to be and ran to the North side window. He flicked on the searchlight and trained the beam along the ground. He relaxed as he saw the camp's Alsatian dog, Tracker, sniffing along the fence.

Panic over, he turned his attention back to the room. He noted with interest that there were three telephones lined up against the wall, which meant he could use one for his own personal use when he was up there on his own.

It was too late to call anybody now; his family would all be asleep, and he was sure that Ellie's mum wouldn't appreciate a call after midnight. He settled for writing her another letter instead. Only, as he started to write, he couldn't think of much else to write, since he had already written to her this morning. Abandoning his pen and paper, he got up and started the search for some food that the last soldier might have left. He found none, but was excited when he discovered a mini fridge that contained some milk. He put the kettle on to boil, and set about making a cup of tea.

A thought struck him, and he went back to the row of computers and studied the screens. The programme that was used here was one he was familiar with, and he decided to set the alarm on the infrared programme. This meant that if an intruder came into camp, the alarm would alert Stu, which meant he wouldn't have to sit and stare at the screens for eight hours. It would work fine, so long as Tracker settled down and didn't keep running all over the camp.

Alarms set and the tea abandoned, Stu made himself comfortable and pulled a rug over his lap. He would be able to have forty winks now. Hell, if the camp was quiet all night, he could at last get a decent night's sleep.

The camp, however, wasn't quiet. The alarm that Stu had set rang shrilly at 0347 hours and he woke at once, bounding out of the chair and over to the screen. For a second he couldn't locate the source of the disturbance, and as he scanned all of the screens he reached out and turned off the alarm. In the quiet he was able to concentrate, and finally he saw it; he, or they, were outside the camp gates. Stu reached for his binoculars and looked out of the window. In the dim lights of the camp, he could just make out three or four figures milling around alongside a car that was parked at the gates. He knew straight away what this meant and, without pause for thought, he ran back to the computer screens. At the same time, he flicked two switches, the alarm that would wake the whole of the barracks and the full beam, so the camp was lit up. He raced to the open hatch and yelled down as the troops piled out of the doors of the barracks.

"Proxy Bomb!"

They all knew what it was when they saw the now abandoned car at the gates, and the camp sprang into action.

Stu, his job to alert the camp now done, went back to the window. Instead of watching the action outside, he turned to the screen, which was now a hive of activity in infrared. He had been warned about the activities of the I.R.A, and this trick seemed to be a favourite. The idea was to drive a vehicle up to the gates of army camps—with the owner of the stolen vehicle normally still in the driving seat—set a bomb off inside the car moments later, destroying some of the camp and killing their victim. Normally the victim would be one of their enemies, or even one of their own who had turned against the I.R.A.

Two birds, one stone.

He could now hear a series of loud noises outside and, as he reached for his binoculars, he realised it was a series of small explosions at the gates.

Stu got his binoculars in focus and trained the spotlight on the car. He clenched his fists as he saw that there indeed was someone strapped into the driver's seat. It was a middle-aged man, and he was yelling at the soldiers who were milling around the car. Panic defined the man's movements as he struggled against the ties that bound him in the death trap.

He heard a shout, and the soldiers scattered seconds before a tiny flame caught at the car's back end with a loud popping sound. The eyes of the man in the driving seat goggled a split second before the car exploded.

Stu lowered his binoculars and took a deep breath. It was the first death that he had witnessed in the army, and he found that he was shaking. That had been a man in there; a man who probably had a wife and children, who certainly had a mother who would now wake up to the R.U.C on her doorstep with the news that her son was now dead, burned alive in a bomb-ridden car, outside an army camp. He realised that he should set the computer screens again; he was still on watch for another two hours, and his job didn't stop just because a bomb had gone off. There could be other attacks, and it was his duty to spot them. He started to walk the perimeter of the room, binoculars trained on all sides of the camp, and, as he walked, a bad feeling started inside him. Things were getting bad here. He didn't think he was going to like Northern Ireland one little bit.

* * * *

Barry woke up and, out of force of habit, turned to look at the clock. It was 4:49 a.m. Oh well, at least he'd gotten four minutes more sleep than the night before.

"Maybe I'm getting better," he muttered as he sat up.

Who're you kidding? the demon hissed and he ignored the voice in his head.

There was no sound from the rest of the house so he dressed quickly and headed downstairs. As he boiled the kettle he flicked the radio on, just in time for the on-the-hour news. He froze, halfway through reaching for a mug, as he listened to the newsreader broadcast the story of the latest attack on the army barracks across town. A thought struck him and he opened the back door and ran down the path to the garden shed. He threw open the door, dropped to his knees at the table and pulled out the boxes that had been stacked there.

The bombs were gone.

Barry put his head in his hands and sat slumped on the cold floor for a long while. He heard Bronwyn calling his name but he stayed still. His heart was thumping in his chest, and it seemed a lifetime before he was able to stagger to his feet and return forlornly to the house.

Bronwyn was at the kitchen table when he shuffled through the door.

"Oh, I thought you'd gone out," she said.

"I did, I mean, no, I didn't," Barry stuttered, his mind still very much on the missing bombs.

"You okay?" she asked.

"Yeah," he said and turned away from her intense stare.

She followed him as he left the room and a frown knitted her brow. Barry was acting awfully strange lately. Normally, if he had a problem she would be the first person he would go to. Not this time, it seemed.

She watched as he shuffled up the stairs and when he reached the top, she called out to him.

"Barry, are you sure you're all right?"

He didn't answer, just lifted a hand in acknowledgement. Moments later she heard his door close quietly.

* * * *

Rosina awoke to her second morning in the Dean house with a feeling of excitement. She had barely slept thinking about Connor coming home and as soon as the sun rose she got out of bed. Mary was in the kitchen, listening to the radio with a grim look on her face.

"Another attack on the barracks," she said as Rosina came into the kitchen. "It's becoming a regular occurrence."

"Was anyone hurt?" asked Rosina.

"A man was tied in his car when they blew it up outside the gates," replied Mary and leaned over to switch the radio off.

Rosina shuddered. Crossmaglen was getting dangerous for everybody it seemed.

"You're up early," commented Mary.

"I couldn't sleep, I'm real excited," said Rosina as she joined Mary at the table.

Mary sat back and regarded the girl with a watchful eye. She had grown quite fond of Rosina, and despite her early misgivings, it seemed like the girl was here to stay.

"If Billy had lived, would you have gone ahead with leaving Ireland?" asked Rosina.

"Yes," replied Mary without a second thought. "There was nothing for us here. We would have lived our lives in Crossmaglen like fugitives."

"Do you think Connor and I will have to leave?"

Mary sighed, it was bound to come up sooner or later and she had been expecting the question.

"That's up to you. Who knows, people might be more tolerant. Then again, they might not. That's a decision you and Connor will have to make."

Rosina nodded and spoke no more about it. But the seed had been planted and, with the frequent attacks and animosity surrounding her relationship, Rosina knew it was going to be something they would have to consider.

Mary interrupted her thoughts. "What do you do, girl? I mean, do you work?"

"Oh. Yes. Well, I'm at college part time, but I work in the council offices in the town. I'm on holiday at the moment but I'm due back on Monday."

"What are you doing at college?" Mary asked.

"Art," said Rosina and blushed.

"Are you any good?"

"I guess so, well, people tell me I am," replied Rosina.

Mary laughed and began to clear away her ashtray and mug. The girl was very modest.

"I'd like to see some stuff you've done, if I can," she said and, since her back was turned, she didn't see the huge smile of gratification on Rosina's face.

* * * *

Connor was dressed and practicing on his crutches when Mary arrived to collect him. A look of panic flitted across his face when he saw that she was alone.

"The girl's at home, love. Don't worry, she's not done a runner. Not yet, anyway."

"And she won't, Ma, at least I hope not," replied Connor.

"Nah, she's here to stay," said Mary and helped him off the bed.

As they walked along the corridor, Connor sneaked a sideways look at his mother.

"You like her, don't you?" he asked.

Mary shrugged.

"Come on, I know you do. I knew you would!" he laughed.

"She's okay, I suppose," Mary said grudgingly. "For a Fenian."

Connor stuck both crutches under his left arm and gave Mary an awkward hug with his right.

"Thanks for looking after her," he said.

Mary said nothing but Connor saw the smile that played around her lips.

She was waiting in the lounge and, when she heard the front door open, she stood up, nervously wringing her hands. Mary discreetly vanished into the kitchen and, as Connor came into the room, he threw aside the crutches and scooped her up into his arms.

"I'm so glad you're home," she said. "How's your leg?"

"Okay." He sat down on the couch, pulling Rosina down with him. "You don't know how good it is to have you here."

"I'm so happy to be here, your mam has been great," Rosina smiled shyly. "I think she likes me."

Connor sat back and took Rosina's hand. How could his mother not like her? How could anybody fail to be taken in by her charm? She was the sweetest girl he had ever known.

"It's going to be fine now," said Connor, as he pulled her close once again.

They were still holding each other when the brick crashed through the front window, landing inches away from their feet. Glass showered them both. Rosina pulled away from Connor and let out a scream. Feet thudded in the hallway as Mary heard the commotion and ran into the room. As soon as she saw what had happened she turned tail and charged out of the front door.

"Bastards!" they heard her yell. Connor stumbled out of the lounge and joined his mother in the front garden.

There was nobody in sight so Connor turned and hobbled back to the lounge.

Rosina sat in the same position on the couch and his eyes widened as he saw that she was covered in glass from the broken window. As she raised her head to look at him, he felt such anger at the frightened, wide-eyed stare she gave him.

Then he saw the blood.

"Christ, you're hurt!" he shouted and went to her side, the glass crunching under his feet.

"Just my hands, I think," she said and turned them palm up.

Angry red streaks criss-crossed her hands and Connor held them gently. He felt her shaking; suddenly all of the emotions of the last few days exploded from within him. He stood up and hurled the crutch he held across the room. As it connected with the far wall, he yelled with such fury that Rosina shrank back in fright.

"Bastards! Fucking, lousy bastards!"

"Connor!" Mary had come in and she grabbed his arm. "Get some salt water and clean up Rosina's hands. I'll get something to cover the window."

Chest heaving and fire dancing in his eyes, Connor ran his hands through his hair as he surveyed the mess around him. He looked down at Rosina who still had not moved and he felt near to tears.

"I'm sorry, Rosie," he said.

"I'm okay, really. I just don't want to get blood on your carpet," she held her hands close to her chest. He felt such love for her at that moment that he would have happily cut his own hands off and given them to her.

"Connor, salt and water," Mary said sternly.

The early afternoon of Connor's homecoming was spent repairing Rosina's hands and the broken window. Mary found a piece of plastic that covered the worst of the shattered glass and got on the telephone to a glazier.

Connor sat at Rosina's feet, with his injured leg stretched out in front of him, carefully picking tiny pieces of glass out of her hands. He had just finished cleaning them free of blood when the phone rang.

"Mam'll get it," Connor said without looking up.

Minutes later, Mary came into the room.

"That was your friend, Bronwyn. She says she'll be in the Felix Bar in an hour."

"Oh, God. I forgot." Rosina looked up at Connor. "She wanted to go for that drink. I should call her and cancel."

"No," Connor spoke quietly but firmly. "We arranged it, and we're going. I'm not going to hide here forever."

"How are your hands?" Mary came over and sat down.

"They're fine," said Rosina.

Connor peered at her palms.

"I think the bleeding is stopping. I'm going to bandage them, 'cause some of these cuts are quite deep. If it doesn't stop, you might need a couple of stitches."

Rosina nodded and looked at the piece of plastic on the window, fluttering in the breeze.

The bleeding would probably stop, but the persecution wouldn't. It would go on and on, until one, or both, or all of them were dead. She and Connor would be victimised, and as long as they stayed in Crossmaglen they would live in fear. If they were to be together, it was time to seriously consider moving for good.

* * * *

Bronwyn put down the telephone and called upstairs for Danny.

He came down and strode into the kitchen.

"So, where're we going? Fox and Hound?" he asked eagerly.

"No, I get enough of that place when I'm at work. No, today we're going to meet a new friend of mine."

Danny pressed her for more information, but Bronwyn would say no more on the subject. She knew that if she told him that they were off to meet Connor, there was no way he would go.

Reluctantly, he tagged along behind her as they walked briskly through the streets of Crossmaglen. When they came to the Divide and Bronwyn continued walking, Danny stopped. She stood a few feet in front of him and turned round.

"Come on!"

"Jesus, Bronwyn, what are you doing going over there?" Danny asked in astonishment.

She tapped her foot impatiently as he walked over to her, nervously looking around.

"Look, Rosina has had to move out of home and all she could get was a place out here. We're going to meet her for a drink and show her she still has friends back home."

"Just Rosina, right?" he asked cautiously.

"Just Rosina," she lied and took his hand. "Now, come on, will you!"

When they walked into the Felix Bar it was almost empty, and Bronwyn felt Danny relax beside her. She spotted Rosina at once and pulled Danny over.

"Hey, Rosie, how you—?" Danny broke off as he noticed the lad sitting next to her.

His gaze fell upon the boy's crutches and he felt the blood drain from his face.

"What happened to your hands?" Bronwyn was talking now and he tried to concentrate on what she was saying.

"What?" he asked, his voice sounding loud and false in his ears.

"Rosina's hands!" Bronwyn said and pulled Danny onto the seat while Rosina explained about the brick incident.

Danny sat down and glanced up to see Connor staring at him.

"Have we met before?" asked Connor.

"No," said Danny, staring down at the table.

"Dan, get a round in, yeah?" Bronwyn nudged him and Danny squeezed out past her, glad to not be sitting opposite the lad he had shot only days earlier.

After checking out everybody's glasses, he went up to the bar.

Connor turned in his seat and watched him go. Bronwyn's boyfriend seemed awfully familiar, but he couldn't work out why. As Danny called back to Rosina to ask if she wanted ice in her drink, Connor frowned. He recognised Danny's voice, too, but, like a dream that faded upon waking, he just couldn't grasp the memory of it.

Danny returned to the table and passed Connor his pint without comment.

"Two diet cokes for the lasses," he said and nudged Bronwyn to move up and along the seat.

You fuckin' leave our lasses alone.

The thought popped into Connor's head and suddenly he knew why Danny was familiar. He looked across to him and broke out in a cold sweat.

"You!" Connor said and the other three looked at him. "It was *you*!"

Danny's eyes widened and Bronwyn knew straight away that Connor had recognised Danny. Rosina looked confused.

"Connor?" she asked and touched his arm.

He shrugged her off and stood up, leaning against the table for support.

"You fuck! How can you sit here and buy me a drink after what you did?" Connor hissed and suddenly Rosina realised what was going on.

"Oh no, oh no, it wasn't, no, no," she said and cast a frantic look at Bronwyn who had turned as red as Danny.

Danny swallowed hard and looked from Rosina to Bronwyn, then back down at the tabletop. He refused to meet Connor's stare.

"I never done anything," he muttered and before anybody could move Danny had fled from the bar.

"Bronwyn? Tell Connor he's wrong, Danny wouldn't shoot anybody, tell him!" cried Rosina as the door slammed after Danny.

Bronwyn said nothing, which gave Rosina her answer, and she balled her hands into fists under the table.

"Oh no, I don't believe he did it! And you! Did you know?" Rosina was angry now. Connor took her clenched fists and wrapped his own hands around hers.

"I didn't know until after!" Bronwyn burst out. "Do you think I would have let him do it if I'd have known before? I'd have died before I let him hurt you."

"Did you tell him about us?" Connor spoke up for the first time.

There was no point lying. Bronwyn was sick and tired of all the lies in her life at the moment.

"Yes, I did," she said. "But I thought I could trust him. Never in a million years did I think he would use it to hurt you two."

She held her breath and watched Rosina's expression.

"I know you didn't do it deliberately. You're my best friend," Rosina said wearily. "It's not your fault."

Bronwyn heaved a sigh of relief. As she watched Connor comfort Rosina, it all suddenly became clear to her. Never in the whole year she had been with Danny could she remember him acting so tenderly to her as the couple before her were. She had convinced herself that it didn't matter, that it wasn't Danny's style. But it was wrong, *she* had been wrong, and it had taken a lot but her eyes had finally been opened.

"What about Danny?" asked Rosina.

"Screw him, he's history," replied Bronwyn and looked down at the table. "I thought I could make a difference. I've been such a fool."

"You tried, and it means a lot that you want to welcome me into your life, with your people. But, Bronwyn, you deserve better." said Connor.

She raised her eyes to meet Connor's and as she did she felt a link, a connection to him, and she realised that she was blushing.

"I gotta go," she said and turned to Rosina. "Forgive me?"

Rosina reached up and enveloped her in a hug.

"There's nothing to forgive. I love you."

Bronwyn pulled away and darted a glance at Connor. He was still staring at her and she muttered a farewell and dashed from the pub.

As the door swung shut behind her, she leaned against the wall and turned her face up to the sky. What the hell had that been? Electricity, that was what it had felt like. She laughed nervously and started to walk back towards her house.

Chapter Ten

Bronwyn meets Stu

It had been a week since the incident in the Felix Bar, and Bronwyn had seen no sight of Danny. She hadn't contacted him, and he had not turned up at her house. Alia had noticed his absence, and she mentioned it to Bronwyn.

"I've not seen Danny lately. Have you two fallen out?"

"Yes, and I'm not going to see him again. He's a bastard, Ma," replied Bronwyn, as she got ready for work at the Fox and Hound.

"Bronwyn!" exclaimed Alia.

"Well, he is, and if he calls I don't want to see him."

"What did he do?" asked Alia.

"He kneecapped Rosie's boyfriend," said Bronwyn and turned round to see her mother's reaction.

Alia clutched her chest and stared hard at her daughter to see if she was joking.

"Are you kidding me, young lady? 'Cause it ain't funny."

"No, I'm not. Connor's walking around on crutches, and it was Danny's doing."

"Jesus, I'd never have thought...you keep away from him, you hear me?" Alia said sternly.

"Well, that's what I just said, Mother. I don't want to see him," said Bronwyn in an exasperated tone. "Will I see you later in the pub?"

"I might pop in. I'm going to call Cally again in America."

Bronwyn laughed at the excitement on her mother's face and hugged her affectionately.

Alia watched Bronwyn leave the house. She worried about her daughter and the company she kept. It was well known that Danny was a fully fledged I.R.A member and, now with Rosina's new boyfriend, it seemed as though Bronwyn always had to be stuck right in the middle of whatever crisis was happening.

* * * *

Stu was halfway up the observation tower, stocking up with some food and tea bags for his shift later that night, when the helicopter came into the camp. He dumped the armful of goodies on the table and, along with Carter who was on watch, went over to the window. When they saw the man get out of the helicopter with a postbag, they made a mad dash for the hatch. By the time they got back to the barracks, the man was handing out the letters and parcels to the other soldiers. He looked up when the two men came in and asked their names.

"Carter and Jackson," said Steve, crossing his fingers.

"One for Carter—" the man shuffled through his pile of post. "—and five for Jackson. Popular guy, huh?" He handed them over and Stu grabbed them eagerly.

He scanned the envelopes and saw that two were from his mother, two were from Ellie, and the other one had handwriting on it that he didn't recognise.

He looked around the busy barracks and decided to find somewhere quieter to devour the mail from home. He made his way out of the door and went over to one of the Sangers on the base. He opened the letter with the writing he didn't recognise, and was pleased to see that it was a Christmas card and letter from his Nan. Not able to wait any longer, he opened the first of Ellie's letters and made himself as comfortable as he could in the cold Sanger.

The first letter was full of news from home and what Ellie had been doing. She mentioned at the bottom that she couldn't wait to see him and asked when he was next due for leave. He put the letter aside and worked out the dates. It was now December 24th. He was due to finish the tour in early August and he would get one week's leave half way through in March. He picked up the letter again and started to read. As far as he was concerned, March couldn't come soon enough.

He was about to start on Ellie's second letter when he heard Carter calling his name outside.

"In here," he called back and sat up as Carter came in.

"Guess what?" said Carter, his face flushed with excitement. "We get to go out tonight. Merry Christmas, mate!"

"Out where?" asked Stu.

"Anywhere. It'll be bloody great just to get out of these bloody barracks. We can go to town, go to a pub!"

"Nice one. How come we're being let out?" asked Stu.

"They say they're expecting trouble over Christmas so there won't be much chance of getting out then, so we get to rip up the town tonight instead."

"What about my shift up there?" Stu nodded towards the observation tower.

"It doesn't start until midnight, does it? We'll be back by then. It just means you just can't get too bladdered!"

With that, Carter left the Sanger, leaving Stu to pack up his letters and get back to the barracks. Between Ellie's letters and this unexpected night out, it was turning out to be a pretty good day after all.

* * * *

The Fox and Hound tended to get pretty packed on a Saturday night, and with tonight being Christmas Eve, it was bound to get the customers in. Bronwyn took advantage of the quiet early evening to make sure the bar was fully stocked. Tonight she was working with two other girls, Kristin and Hannah. They were both slightly older than she was, and the three always got on well whenever they were put on shift together. Just after six o'clock, somebody started banging on the doors and Bronwyn raised her eyes.

"Time to open, I guess," she said, throwing the bunch of keys at Kristin.

As the doors opened, a group of about seven men barged in, making their way up to the bar. Bronwyn greeted them all by their first names; they were men she had known for years, and to her they were old friends.

Bronwyn was one of the most popular barmaids in the Fox. She took the time to listen to the punters, and she knew what all of her regulars drank without having to ask them.

"Okay," said Bronwyn and narrowed her eyes as she looked over each of the seven men in front of her. "Three whiskeys, large, a lime and soda, two pints of Guinness, and a bitter. Am I right?"

The men cheered and applauded. It was a game she played with all of her regulars, and it was a rare occasion that her memory served her wrong.

Bronwyn served them quickly; the bar was starting to fill now and, as she turned to serve the next customer, she was aghast to see Danny standing at the bar, holding his money up in the air with a smirk on his face.

She took a deep breath and fixed her 'barmaid's smile' onto her face.

"Evening, what'll it be?" she asked.

"Whiskey, no ice. Make it a double," he replied. "And one for yourself."

"I'm fine, thank you," she said, serving him quickly.

She turned to serve her next customer, thinking it was over, until he spoke again.

"I've missed you," he said.

Bronwyn wavered. Should she ignore him? After all, she was at work now and didn't want any trouble from him during her shift. Deciding to pretend she hadn't heard him, she went to the next customer at the bar.

A glance over her shoulder showed that Danny had retreated from the bar, and she was relieved.

"Kristin, if Danny comes back, can you serve him?" she asked.

Kristin agreed, and for the next couple of hours they worked non-stop. Just after seven, Bronwyn said that she was going for her break and made her way into the back.

Stu, sitting to the left of the bar in the Fox and Hound, had had his eye on Bronwyn since he had arrived. She was by far the most striking girl he had seen since—well—since Ellie. Thoughts of Ellie crossed his mind followed by a sudden attack of guilt. What was he doing, sitting here eyeing up another girl, when he had Ellie waiting at home for him? He turned to Carter and tried to focus on what he was saying, when a guy staggering past him pushed him roughly to one side.

"Hey, watch it!" he said, trying to balance his pint.

The lad didn't answer him, and Stu frowned as he saw him following the girl behind the bar as she went out of a side door.

Bronwyn opened the door that led to the back alley, breathing in the clean air. Suddenly, she heard a loud crash and she turned, startled, to see Danny stagger through the door into the room.

"Danny! You can't be in here," she said. "Get out!"

"Not until you listen to me. I need you back. Let's talk about it, yeah?" he slurred. Bronwyn realised he had had a lot more than the one whiskey she had served him.

"I'm working, and there's nothing to talk about. I don't want you anymore," she replied. "Now, either go back in the bar, or go home."

He didn't move and, for the first time since she had known him, she began to feel slightly frightened of him.

"Danny, go!" she said.

He moved quickly, storming over to her. His hand flew out, grabbing her by the throat. She emitted a squeak and grabbed onto his arms as he forced her through the open door and into the alley. She grunted in pain as he smashed her back against the wall. Frantically she looked around for help. She saw his fist coming and, as it smashed into the side of her face, she saw stars.

Suddenly a shape loomed up from her right side and smashed into Danny. Danny let go of her. She slumped down on the ground and put her hand to her face where Danny had hit her. She looked up and saw a man of about her age, he looked tall to her but that may just have been how it looked from her vantage point on the ground. His hair was shaved close to his head and his blue eyes glinted with fury as he landed a punch to Danny's jaw. With Danny immobilised, the man turned his attention to Bronwyn.

"Are you okay?" he asked.

"I am now," she said and realised she was shaking. "Who are you?"

"Stu. Stuart Jackson" he said and, as he moved into the light, she smiled at him.

"I'm Bronwyn and that cretin is my boyfriend."

"Boyfriend?" he asked, raising his eyebrows.

Bronwyn studied Danny as he clutched at his nose, which had blood pouring from it.

"Well, ex-boyfriend, actually."

"Glad to hear that," Stu said. "Um, your eye looks pretty sore. Do you want me to get some ice?"

"No, I think I'd better go home," Bronwyn shivered in the cold night air.

"At least let me walk you. I insist," said Stu.

She looked him up and down, trying to work out where he was from. With his accent he obviously wasn't Irish. Before she could ask, Danny rose up and, with a yell, made once more for Bronwyn. This time she was ready for him and before Stu could react, she doubled him up with a blow to his stomach. He doubled over, gasping for air. Seeing red, Bronwyn grabbed his hair and pulled him up to face her.

"Leave me alone. Don't ring me or come to my house or you'll get more of the same. Now, fuck off!" she roared.

"Bitch!" he whispered, still wheezing.

"Oh, and Danny…you're barred."

With that, she flounced back inside with a mightily impressed Stu in tow. She slammed the door shut and bolted it behind them.

She was shaking more than ever now and, as she grabbed her coat and bag, she turned to Stu.

"Thank you for helping me, but I'll be fine now."

"Do you live anywhere near the army barracks?" he asked as he followed her through to the bar.

"Yeah, not far. Why?" Her eyes widened and she suddenly burst out laughing. "Oh, don't tell me. You're a soldier?"

"Yeah, I have to be back there by midnight so, if it's on your way, you can walk with me," he replied.

Still laughing at the thought of how mad Danny would be if he knew Stu was a soldier, she agreed that he could walk with her.

* * * *

Across town, Connor and Rosina sat in a small Italian restaurant, looking over the menu for dessert. It had been Connor's idea to come here, and Rosina liked the intimate feel of the place.

"Can we make this a regular thing?" she asked.

"Sure," he answered. "Do you know what dessert you want?"

"Hmm…I'll have the cherry pie," she said, closing the menu.

Once the waiter had taken their order, Connor stood up.

"Back in a sec." He limped off in the direction of the men's room.

Rosina sat back and looked around. They had traveled out of Crossmaglen to Castleblayney, and it was nice to be able to relax for the evening. Nobody knew them here and they faced no hassle about their relationship. Rosina looked down at her hands. The bandages were off and the scars were already fading, just like the memory of what she thought of as her former life.

Connor came back to the table and as he sat down he took her hand.

"I'm real glad you're staying with me," he said. "No regrets?"

She looked into his dark eyes and smiled. "None," she replied.

"'Cause we're forever, you know that?" he asked earnestly.

"I know, but I like to hear you say it." She gave his hand a squeeze.

"Oh, that was quick," said Connor moments later as he caught sight of their waiter coming towards them with a tray.

"Excellent," Rosina said. She waited patiently as the waiter put Connor's dish down in front of him.

"Oh, this looks good," said Rosina as her dessert was placed in front of her.

The waiter left and Rosina picked up the spoon, digging deep into the cherry-filled pie. Only there was something odd about it.

"Connor, there's no cherries in my pie!" she said and looked up at him.

He stabbed into his own pie and came up with a spoonful of cherries.

"I got plenty in mine," he said and gestured to her plate. "Surely there's some in there somewhere."

She dug her spoon in again and gasped as the spoon connected with something hard.

Glancing up to make sure nobody was watching, she put the spoon down and pulled the pastry apart with her fingers. Nestled inside the pie was a small blue box.

"Connor!" She picked it out of the empty pie and looked up just in time to see Connor kneeling awkwardly on the floor.

He reached out to steady himself on the table, wincing at the pain in his knee, then looked up at her.

"Marry me?" he asked.

Rosina gasped in astonishment. When she tried to speak no words came out. She looked back to the box in her now shaking hands and carefully opened it to see a sapphire ring inside.

"Rosie," Connor said, clearing his throat. "I don't know how much longer I can stay down here."

Suddenly she found her power of speech and she grabbed his hand.

"Yes!" she shouted, pulling him up and hugging him hard. "Yes, I'll marry you!"

Their fellow diners, watching the scene unfold, broke into spontaneous applause and their waiter, who had been waiting discreetly, came over with a tray of champagne.

Rosina fell back into her seat and slipped the ring on her finger.

"I can't believe this…did you have all this planned?" she asked.

"Of course," he replied. "It took some talking to get them to make you a pie with no filling in it!"

I'll bet. Oh, Connor, you don't know how happy I am." Tears filled her eyes as she leaned over the table to kiss him. "I love you."

Later, as they walked to the taxi rank, Rosina stopped and turned to Connor.

"What would you have done if I'd ordered a different dessert? Ice cream, say?"

"Oh, well, babe, I know your tastes too well, see," he replied.

She laughed along with him, for the first time feeling confident they would get through the hatred that they faced, and they would come out of the other side stronger than ever.

* * * *

When they arrived at the army barracks, Bronwyn stopped and looked at her watch.

"Right on time," she said.

It was close to midnight and Stu wasn't looking forward to another eight hours stuck in the tower.

Bronwyn wandered up to the gate and looked at the flowers that had been laid in the memory of the man who had died there a week ago.

"Were you here when it happened?" she asked Stu.

"Yeah, I was the one who spotted it and called the alarm."

She shuddered and turned away from the shrine of the man whom she hadn't known.

"Well, thanks for walking me. Maybe I'll see you in the bar again?"

He nodded and watched her walk away. She stopped and turned towards him.

"Merry Christmas!" she called and started to walk again.

He was still standing there when the beam came on from the tower and he turned around.

"Come on, Jackson!" he heard someone up the tower call. He raised his hand in acknowledgement and went into camp.

As soon as he was alone in the tower, Stu switched on the infrared alarms and sat back to mull over the events of the evening. Bronwyn had handled herself well in the wake of her boyfriend's attack, and he had liked her a lot. Standing up and making sure that there was no activity on the screen, he made his way over to the bank of phones on the far wall. It was late to make telephone calls but he felt the need to speak to Ellie, maybe to wash away the impure thoughts of Bronwyn.

He had Ellie's telephone number memorised and he dialed it, keeping one eye on the computer all the time.

"Hello?"

His heart did a little jig as it always did when he heard her voice, and he pulled over the chair he had just vacated.

"Hiya, it's me," he said.

They spoke for two hours, about everything and nothing. Bearing in mind that they didn't really know each other, were just two strangers who had liked the look of each other, there was a lot to do in the 'getting to know you' department.

When Stu spotted a movement on the screen he leapt up from the chair.

"Ellie, I gotta go," he said and hung up the phone.

He raced over to the window and flicked the beam on full. He could see a couple of shapes out there by the fence but, thankfully, no car had been driven up to the gates. He flipped the switch that triggered the alarm and within seconds the camp was a hive of activity. He watched anxiously from the window as half a dozen men ran out of the barracks towards the gates.

"Why does it have to be when I'm on duty?" he whispered to himself. "Gimme a break."

* * * *

When Bronwyn arrived home she wondered if she could sneak upstairs without her mother or brother witnessing the rapidly swelling bruise on her face. Glancing in the mirror as she slipped in the front door, she realized the bruise wasn't going to fade any time soon and she might as well get it over with. As she entered the lounge, both Alia and Barry turned around, their expressions quickly changing to shock when they saw the state of her face.

"What happened?" they cried out simultaneously.

On the walk home with Stu, she had been so distracted by his company that she had almost forgotten about her black eye. Now it throbbed as if to remind her and she lifted her hand to it.

"Danny done it," she said sullenly.

Barry stood up, his face like thunder.

"Where is the bastard?" he asked as he reached for his coat.

"No, Barry." Bronwyn stopped him as he attempted to get past her. "I sorted it. It's over, okay?"

"Fucking hell, Bronwyn, you can't let him get away with this!" yelled Barry.

"I didn't! I just told you it's sorted, so leave it!" she shouted back.

Alia pulled the warring siblings apart and pushed them both on the couch.

"Stop shouting at each other!" she snapped and turned to Bronwyn. "If I see you with that boy again I'll give you a black eye myself."

"It's done! It's fucking finished, like I keep saying!" exclaimed Bronwyn. "Let's just forget about it all right?"

She turned to include Barry and he nodded and sat back, his eyes fixed firmly on the television.

Chapter Eleven

Rosina and Barry's Decline

Christmas day dawned early for Barry. He had managed to stay awake in front of the television until 2:45 a.m. Now, he was awake. He turned over to look at the clock and was aghast to see it was 4:30 a.m. He'd had less than two hours sleep.

Brilliant.

That was one experiment he wouldn't be trying again.

Knowing that there was no point in trying to get back to sleep, Barry decided to go out for a jog. Prior to becoming an informer he had been heavily into fitness, but lately he had been letting that slide. As he dressed, he realised that he felt strangely refreshed. Maybe a couple of hours' sleep was all he needed; after all, Margaret Thatcher existed on only six hours sleep a night.

Who are you kidding? said the voice.

"Shut up," he said, pulling on his jacket.

Half a mile across town, Barry's day took a turn for the worse. He stopped jogging as he saw a man across the road standing at the bus stop, reading a paper. It was Christmas day; there were no buses for the man to be waiting for. His heart began to flutter and he gripped at his chest.

"Jesus," he croaked breathlessly and stumbled on past.

Was someone watching him? Had Andy sent him? Or, was he one of Johnny's henchmen?

His heart rate was almost back to normal when a white Ford Escort cruised slowly past him, the driver turning his head to look at Barry.

Barry straightened up and turned back towards home, his heart throbbing against his rib cage, the sound of his feet pounding the pavement echoing in his ears as he broke into a run. All of a sudden it seemed as if every person on the street was watching him and he moaned as he ran along.

When he reached home he crashed through the door and slammed it shut. He closed his eyes and leaned against it, breathing heavily.

"Barry? Is that you, love?" Alia came out into the hall, holding a ten-pound turkey on a baking tray.

Barry stared at the turkey and cringed back against the door. Who had sent the turkey to spy on him?

Suddenly his vision cleared, and he almost laughed out loud at the absurdity of that thought. Turkeys couldn't spy, especially not one that was skinned and headless on a baking tray.

It might be bugged. The voice spoke up and Barry balled his hands into fists and banged both sides of his head.

"Shut *up!*" he muttered.

"Barry!" Alia was staring at him. "Don't tell me to shut up!"

"Oh no…" Barry went towards her with his hands outstretched. "Not you, Ma. I wasn't talking to you…"

"Well, I don't see anyone else here!" she said and stared, waiting for an explanation.

He started to gesture to the turkey and then thought better of it.

"Never mind," he said. "Can I help you?"

"If you like, the potatoes need peeling," Alia said as she disappeared back to the kitchen.

Barry took a moment to get himself together before he followed her.

* * * *

Stu watched the sun rise from the tower on Christmas morning and felt a wave of depression wash over him. What a lousy place to be spending Christmas. He checked his watch and saw it was only six o'clock; still another two hours to go. At least the rest of the night had been free from unwelcome visitors, after the other soldiers had chased away the intruders.

The hatch opening startled him, and Carter hauled himself up into the room.

"Merry Christmas," Carter said, putting a bottle of brandy on the table.

"Hey, cheers, mate." Stu picked up the bottle and poured a hefty shot into two mugs. "How in hell do you manage to stay so cheerful? I mean, it's Christmas day and we're stuck here."

"Well, when you ain't got nobody pining for you at home, it's just another day." He clinked his mug against Stu's. "But anyway, what happened to you last night? Did ya get lucky?"

Stu laughed and pondered the question.

"I don't know," he said thoughtfully. "But anyway, Happy Christmas to you too, mate."

* * * *

Rosina woke up early to the smell of the bird roasting in the oven and smiled to herself as she pulled her hand out from under the quilt to look at the ring on her finger. What a wonderful Christmas present that had been. She heard Connor and Mary talking in the kitchen, so she jumped out of bed and grabbed the parcels that she had collected the day before.

When she got to the kitchen, she stopped in the doorway to watch Connor and his mother laughing together. She felt a moment of sadness as she realised that this was what a normal family should be like, not the cold and lonely twenty-odd years she had spent with her mother. They spotted her then, and Connor's face lit up as it always did when he saw her.

"Hey!" He reached out and pulled her into the room. "Merry Christmas."

She returned his kiss and turned to Mary.

"Merry Christmas," she said shyly, handing her a wrapped parcel.

"Goodness." Mary took it and smiled. "Come on, let the turkey be, and let's get these gifts unwrapped!"

They retired to the lounge where Connor promptly handed out all of the gifts that had appeared, as if by magic, under the tree. Mary unwrapped her gift from Rosina and smiled at the red dressing gown. It had a monogram of Mary's initials on it. Mary immediately wrapped it around herself.

"It's perfect," she said, looking warmly at Rosina. "Thank you."

"It's real nice, Rosie," said Connor, casting a mischievous glance at his mother. "She does spend most of her time in her dressing gown."

Mary swiped at Connor playfully.

"Cheeky git," she said. "Anyway, Connor, what have you got Rosina?"

Rosina and Connor exchanged glances and Connor moved onto the couch next to Rosina.

"Show her," he said.

Rosina held out her left hand.

Mary gasped and took Rosina's hand for a closer look.

"Oh, Connor," she said and shook her head. "You don't do things by half, do you?"

She smiled but her expression was sad, wistful, and worried, all at the same time.

Rosina knew that Mary was thinking about her own lost love and curled her fingers around Mary's. Mary pulled herself out of her reverie and squeezed Rosina's hand.

"I'm pleased. God help me, and God help you two. I can't believe I'm saying it, but I am pleased."

Rosina nodded and turned back to Connor, dropping her present into his lap.

"It's not a patch on this, I'm afraid," she said and waved her hand at him, admiring the way the sapphire gleamed in its gold setting.

Connor eagerly ripped the wrapping away and opened the box to reveal a white gold bracelet. He held it up and pulled Rosina to him.

"I love it," he said, studying it. "Oh, it's engraved!"

"What does it say?" asked Mary.

"Connor and Rosina, forever," he read it out before slipping the bracelet on. "This is the best Christmas ever!"

Later, as Connor sat in the lounge and Rosina helped Mary to clear away the dinner plates, she thought about Kathleen.

"I have to see my mother," she said suddenly.

"Well, I'm sure she'd like to see you, too, today of all days," replied Mary.

"No, I mean, if me and Connor are going to be married, I'll need my birth certificate, won't I?"

"Oh, well, yes, you probably will." She touched Rosina's arm. "Why don't you see her anyway? Today is a day for forgiveness and peace, after all."

Rosina nodded and thought about it. The certificate she would need, and Mary was right, today was as good a day as any to extend the olive branch.

Before she could change her mind, she dried her hands on the tea towel and went to tell Connor where she was going.

When she saw that he was sleeping, she crept out again and said goodbye to Mary.

"Good luck," said Mary and watched her leave.

It took twenty minutes to walk back to her old home and she grew more nervous with every step that she took. When she found herself standing on the doorstep, she almost fled with the fear of facing her mother again. But she steeled herself, thought of her pending wedding, and rapped hard on the door.

Kathleen opened the door, glass of sherry in one hand and an almost empty bottle in the other.

"My baby girl!" she exclaimed and raised her arms up in a welcoming gesture, not noticing the sherry that slopped over the edge of the glass and onto the carpet.

Rosina cringed. She had never seen her mother drunk, and, in fact, Kathleen had never shown herself to be anything other than in complete control.

"Mam, can I come in?" she asked, edging through the door.

"What in hell is that?" Kathleen barked suddenly, making Rosina jump.

She realised that her mother was looking at the ring on her finger and she guiltily put her hands in her pockets.

"Oh, that, er...that's sort of why I'm here," she replied.

"Jesus Christ, you're gonna marry the bastard!" Kathleen said with a look of incredulity on her face. "Good luck, sweetheart, you're gonna need it."

With that, Kathleen staggered off down the hall, leaving Rosina with no choice but to follow her.

"See, Mam, it's my birth certificate I need. To apply for a marriage licence," she called after her mother.

Kathleen slumped into her chair and regarded Rosina with narrowed eyes.

"And why the hell would I give you anything you ask for?" she said and poured another sherry.

Rosina felt on the verge of tears as she looked around the house that she used to call home. How very different it was to Connor's home, or Bronwyn's. No Christmas decorations adorned the house, no bird in the oven, in fact there was nothing here to say it was the festive season at all.

"I'll just find it myself then," Rosina said quietly and made her way into the front room.

Where to start? She knew where Kathleen kept all of her important papers; it was an old shoebox, blue in colour if she remembered correctly, but where Kathleen kept the box itself was anybody's guess. She started on the sideboard, and the third drawer down proved successful as Rosina pulled out the shoebox. She sat on the carpet and opened it up, spilling all the papers it contained onto the floor. Finally, she located a birth certificate and she picked it up to make sure it was hers, and not her mother's. It was. Her name, Rosina James, mother's name…well, that was strange. The father's name was blank.

Rosina stood up and looked over the piece of paper again. Why wouldn't Kathleen have put her father's name on the certificate? She put the rest of the papers back in the box and placed the box back where she had found it. Still clutching the certificate, she went back into the kitchen.

"Mam?" she asked and pulled a chair up opposite her mother. "Why is my father's name not on this?"

Kathleen flinched as if she had been punched as she looked up at Rosina.

"What are you doing with that?" she whispered.

"I told you, I need it for a marriage license. Answer me, Mam, why is it blank here where my father's name should be?"

Kathleen stood up, her chair scraping on the tiled floor as she clutched at her chest.

"You shouldn't have gone through my things! You should have left it alone!"

Rosina had a strange feeling. This was something new, something about her past that she didn't know, and she stood up so she was on the same level as her mother.

"What's going on here?" she asked, her voice sounding stronger than she actually felt.

"You have no father," Kathleen said without expression.

Rosina laughed and shook her head.

"Everybody has a father. There was only one Immaculate Conception, and it wasn't me." A thought struck her and she stared at Kathleen. "Are you telling me he's not dead?"

Kathleen sagged against the counter behind her.

"I don't know," she said quietly.

"What? What do you mean?" Rosina realised that she was shaking and she waved the certificate in the air. "Tell me what the hell is going on. This is obviously something you've kept from me all my life. I have a right to know!"

She was shouting now. Suddenly Kathleen slammed her hands down on the table and hissed out words that would change Rosina's life as she knew it.

"I was raped!" Kathleen spat the words out. "I was raped, and you were the result, you…you…devil's spawn!"

Rosina sat down heavily and her mouth fell open in shock. It all became clear; the way her mother had treated her all of her life, never showing love or affection to her.

"You're lying," she said, voice trembling, hoping—desperately wishing—that it were just a lie, just another way for her mother to hurt her.

Kathleen shook her head and her eyes flashed angrily as all of the emotions she had kept hidden for the past twenty-one years came pouring out of her in one livid flood of hateful words.

"He raped me, and took away my life, and left me with you! I hated you from the moment you were born, and that never went away. I should have taken my mother's advice and got rid of you!"

Kathleen drew in a sharp breath when she realised what she had said and clapped her hand to her mouth as if to stop another torrent of abuse escaping.

"Why didn't you get rid of me?" Rosina asked, her eyes shining with unshed tears.

"I thought it would be different. I thought you would be more mine than *his*," Kathleen said miserably.

"And you never loved me, not for a second," Rosina sounded so sad that Kathleen regretted her harsh words.

"I did love you, I do," she said and paused. "I tried to love you."

"That's another lie!" Rosina stood up, the certificate falling to the floor.

Kathleen, the enormity of what she had done hitting her, slumped down to the floor and wrapped her arms around herself.

Rosina turned and walked out of the house without looking back.

As she closed the door behind her, she heard her mother wail from the kitchen and she shivered. It was the sound of an animal in terrible pain, and she staggered away from the house, down to the gate. At the gate, she looked back and tears filled her eyes. Her throat felt raw and a moan escaped from deep inside her.

My father – a rapist!

As the thought crossed her mind, Rosina gagged and stumbled out of the garden and into the road. When she reached the gutter she leaned over and threw up the dinner she had eaten hours earlier. When she had finished she got back onto the pavement and held onto a lamppost for support.

Suddenly the door opened, and Rosina looked up to see Kathleen illuminated by the light of the hall.

"Rosina?" Kathleen called out into the street.

Rosina didn't answer, instead she forced her feet to walk further onto the pavement, and clinging to the gardens walls and fences she started the long walk back to Connor.

When Rosina crashed through the front door of Mary's house she was on the verge of collapse. She had cried all the way home, sobbing and retching uncontrollably, as she walked along. Connor came out into the hall and he hobbled over to where she was bent double by the front door.

"Rosina, hey, hey!" He panicked and put his arms around her. "What's happened, did someone hurt you?"

She shook her head and Connor watched helplessly as the tears continued to course down her face.

"Was it your ma?" he asked, quieter now, and she nodded, the tears falling from her face like droplets of rain.

"Mam!" he called. "Something's wrong with Rosie, come here!"

Mary came running and taking one look at Rosina she hauled the girl up and pulled her into the lounge. Mary clasped Rosina's hands tight between hers and looked up at Connor.

"She's had one helluva shock. I bet her mother's upset her again." She turned her attention back to Rosina. "Can you tell us what happened?"

Rosina clutched Mary's hand and stared, wide-eyed, at the pair of them. They wanted her to tell them what had upset her so, but she felt so ashamed by the truth of her parentage she couldn't face it.

"Okay, no pressure. Connor, you go and get me some whiskey and a blanket. This girl's as cold as ice," Mary instructed Connor and he turned and hurried out.

When he had gone, Mary turned to Rosina.

"Do you want to tell me what happened?"

With Connor gone it was easier somehow, and she managed to get her weeping under control as she recounted the story to Mary.

"She must be lying," said Mary when Rosina had finished.

"No, I know it was true. I wish I didn't know. I feel...dirty." With that, fresh tears rolled down Rosina's cheeks and Mary enveloped her in a hug.

"You're not—it's not your fault, girl," she whispered and felt tears sting her own eyes as the girl clung onto her as if she were drowning.

Connor came back and gave his mother a questioning look. She shook her head and he retreated from the room.

It seemed like hours later when Rosina slumped against Mary and she realised that the girl had fallen asleep. Mary gently covered her with the blanket that Connor had left and went into the kitchen where Connor was waiting.

"She's asleep," Mary said and looked at the whiskey bottle that she was still holding. "Think I could do with some of this."

"What's wrong with her?" asked Connor in hushed tones.

Mary took a deep breath and told Connor everything that Rosina had told her. Connor was white-faced as he listened and, when Mary finished, he stood up to go to her.

"Leave her." Mary put her hand out and clutched Connor's arm. "She needs to rest."

Connor sat down and put his head in his hands.

"This is all going to be tough, Connor," said Mary. "Are you sure you want to do this? That poor girl is going to be in turmoil for a long while."

"Of course," exclaimed Connor. "I love her!"

Mary nodded and covered Connor's hand with her own.

"You love her, lad, I've no doubt of that. But, Connor…are you *in* love with her?"

Connor laughed. "What a strange question!"

"But how do you feel about her? Tell me," demanded Mary.

"I told you, I love her. I want to protect her," replied Connor. "What's this all about?"

Mary hesitated before answering. "It's important to have passion."

Connor laughed, more out of embarrassment than humour.

No, listen, lad. I can see you love her, and of course you do, she's the sweetest girl I've met and you've the biggest heart in this county. But you can't be with her to protect her, not solely, anyway."

Warning bells sounded in Connor's head and he paled slightly.

Seeing that her words had made some sort of impact, Mary stood up and collected up the empty mugs.

Connor wrapped the tablecloth around his fingers, a frown of concentration knitting his brow.

Could there be any truth in his mother's words?

* * * *

Alia, Bronwyn, and Barry sat down to their Christmas dinner, each lost in their own thoughts. It was a quiet, somber affair, most unlike the normal rowdiness of the Ranger household. After the meal was finished and the gifts had been opened, Bronwyn stood up.

"I'm popping out for a while. I won't be too long," she said.

Before she left, she went into the kitchen and wrapped up some of the leftover food, along with a hefty slice of the so far untouched Christmas cake.

It was bitterly cold outside and she wrapped her coat tight around her as she hurried along the deserted streets towards the army barracks.

When she arrived at the gates there were a couple of soldiers milling around and she called out to them. They looked up and one of them wandered over to her.

"Do you know Stuart?" she asked.

"Stu Jackson? Yeah, want me to get him?"

"Please," she said and waited while the soldier went off towards the barracks.

Moments later Stu came out and when he saw her he jogged over to the gate to let himself out.

"I just brought you these," she said, handing him the package.

He took it and a smile lit up his face as he pulled back the tinfoil she had wrapped the food in.

"Wow, thank you," he said. "This is great."

"I thought you could make use of this, too." She pulled a bottle of Irish liqueur out of her coat.

"You didn't have to do this," he said. "But I'm grateful. We don't get anything like this in here."

"It's to say thank you, for helping me last night." She turned to go.

"Wait!" he called after her.

She turned back again.

"Can I see you again?" he asked.

"Sure," she said and for a moment they stood in silence, smiling at each other.

"Soon," Stu said.

She nodded and shoving her hands deep in her pockets, she walked off down the lane.

Stu let himself back into the barracks and looked once more at the food she had given him. He didn't know what had possessed him to ask her out, and he felt slightly guilty about it. He couldn't kid himself that he was just interested in her as a friend either. Pushing the worries out of his mind, he went in search of Carter to see if he wanted to share the food.

* * * *

Boxing Day dawned and Bronwyn awoke confused from a half-forgotten dream about Connor and Stu. She didn't know what it was about Stu, but he had been on her mind frequently since her visit to the barracks yesterday. She got up and opened the curtains, feeling a childlike excitement when she saw it had snowed during the night. Then she saw Barry in the garden and she tapped on the window. He didn't hear her; he was engrossed in whatever he was doing.

"What *is* he doing?" she said to herself as she watched him walk around the shed, looking as though he had lost something.

Pulling on her dressing gown, she went downstairs and out the back door.

"Barry?" she called. "What are you doing?"

He jumped when he heard her and spun around, a wild look on his face.

"Bronwyn?" he peered at her. "Is that you?"

"Of course. Who did you think it was, your I.R.A mates come to get you?" she was joking, but his eyes widened in fear at her words.

"Are they here?" he asked. Walking backwards, he stumbled around the back of the shed.

"No, I was joking." She followed him and came around the corner of the shed. "Barry, are you in some kind of trouble?"

"Tell them I'm not here, tell them I've left!" he was babbling now and he flapped his hands at her. "Go, before they come out here!"

Bronwyn knew something was very wrong and she reached out to catch hold of his hands.

"Barry, nobody is here. Just you, Ma, and me. That's all."

She watched as his expression changed from one of confusion to clarity.

"Sorry, sis. Think I must still be drunk from last night," he said.

"You didn't drink last night. You stayed in, with us," she replied.

He didn't respond to this, instead he moved past her and out into the open garden.

She watched as he returned to the house and shook her head. Something was wrong with Barry. Drugs, maybe? No, Barry wasn't into that and, if he were, she would know about it.

Suddenly she heard her mother calling her from the house so she came back into the kitchen.

"Bronwyn, that Connor's on the phone and he doesn't sound very good," she said.

Bronwyn frowned and going into the hall, she picked up the phone.

Alia leaned back against the kitchen door and listened in on Bronwyn's side of the telephone conversation.

"Connor…what…slow down…" Bronwyn cast a worried look at Alia and nodded as she listened to him.

Suddenly her face turned white, she clutched the phone, and held her hand out in a subconscious gesture to her mother. Alia hurried over and waited while Bronwyn hung up the phone and turned to her mother, ashen faced.

"What is it? Is it Rosie?" Alia asked.

"Oh, my God, Ma, this is bad," said Bronwyn.

"What is? Has something happened to her?"

Bronwyn talked as she gathered her coat and bag together.

"Apparently, Rosina went to her mother's yesterday, something about getting her birth certificate, and when she questioned Kathleen about her father, Kathleen said she didn't know his name. He's not dead. He raped her and she got pregnant!"

"Good God!" Alia crossed herself.

"Rosie's distraught. I've got to get over there," said Bronwyn. "Ma, when I'm gone will you keep an eye on Barry for me? Something's up with him."

Alia watched Bronwyn leave the house and pondered upon Bronwyn's words. She had noticed that there was something up with Barry, but, unlike Bronwyn, he was a closed book, and unless he wanted to talk about whatever was troubling him, there would be no point in asking.

* * * *

Barry sat on the windowsill of his bedroom and watched Bronwyn leave the house. He gripped the curtain, watching in terror as five or six men, all wearing black suits, came out of the shadows and started to follow his sister.

"Leave her alone!" he cried and banged on the window.

But the men paid no heed to his plea.

They didn't listen because they were not really there. The men who had been stalking him, and were now following Bronwyn, existed only in Barry's mind.

* * * *

When Bronwyn arrived at Connor's house, he was sitting on the front step. He looked up as she approached. She sat down next to him to catch her breath after running most of the way across town.

"What happened to your face?" he asked as he studied her black eye.

"Oh, Danny," she replied. "It's no big deal."

"He's a fucking lunatic, Bronwyn. You should stay away from him."

"I intend to from now on. How's Rosie?" she asked.

"Not good. She's in bed, won't get up, won't talk or even cry. She's just sitting there," he replied, looking up at her.

She felt a huge amount of pity for him when she saw the pain in his eyes.

"I can't believe it. I've known her my whole life, and her bitch mother as well. I can't understand what made Kathleen so mad to tell Rosie this."

"I think it was me," said Connor and kicked at the crutch lying at his feet. "Rosie said when Kathleen saw the ring she went mental."

"Ring?" Bronwyn was confused.

Connor smiled and for a second a look of joy dispelled his serious expression.

"I asked her to marry me," he said.

For one moment, just one split second, Bronwyn was devastated. The feeling shocked her for she had no reason to feel that way, but she quickly painted a smile on her face and Connor took her shaken expression for one of joyful surprise.

"Congratulations, you two belong together," she replied.

He looked at her then, faces inches apart, and it seemed to Bronwyn that he looked right into her and saw every part of who she was. There was an awkward silence, then the moment passed and Bronwyn stood up, dusting off her jeans.

"Can I see her?" she asked, not looking at him.

"Sure." A flush spread over his handsome face and he leaned back and pushed open the door.

She hurried in, running up the stairs as if to flee from whatever had happened back there at the door. When she opened one of the doors upstairs and looked into the room, all thoughts of Connor vanished as she saw Rosina sitting in the bed, wide eyes staring at nothing in particular, looking very small and fragile in the large bed.

"Oh, Rosie," she spoke from the doorway and Rosina looked up, startled.

When she saw Bronwyn, her face crumpled and she held out her arms in a gesture a child would use to beckon her mother.

Bronwyn ran over to the bed and held Rosina as a fresh torrent of tears started.

"What can I do? Is there anything I can do?" asked Bronwyn.

Rosina pulled away and grabbed a crumpled tissue off an already large pile on the bedside table.

"Nobody can do anything. I wish I didn't know," Rosina wailed.

"But you do know, and you have to deal with it, then leave it alone."

"I know, but he…" Rosina trailed off and glanced around the room before leaning in close to Bronwyn. "He raped her!

How can I forget that? Nobody would ever want me, knowing that I'm a product of a rape!"

Bronwyn gripped Rosina's shoulders and shook her hard.

"Connor wants you! He asked you to marry him, you bloody lucky cow!" Despite her true feelings, Bronwyn couldn't help smiling at the thought of little Rosina James getting married.

Rosina brightened for a moment and she opened the drawer of her bedside table to retrieve the engagement ring. Bronwyn took it and admired the sparkling sapphire.

"Beautiful. But, Rosie, you should be wearing it." Bronwyn caught hold of Rosina's hand and tried to put the ring on.

Rosina grabbed it with her right hand and put it back in the drawer. A frown crossed her pretty face and she looked down at the floor.

"I don't feel I should be wearing it. I don't think I deserve to wear it."

"But Rosie—"

"No, Bronwyn," Rosina interrupted. "I feel like I'm not me anymore. Connor's such a good person, and he loved what he thought I was. He doesn't want *this* me—this dirty, unclean me."

"Oh, Jesus, Rosina, that's not true. I just saw him outside, and when he told me that he'd asked you to marry him, his face lit up like a bloody Christmas tree!"

Rosina smiled and for a moment Bronwyn thought she'd gotten through to her friend.

"Connor's too decent to go back on his word now. It might be easier if I left him."

"Easier for who? Not him. You'll break his heart!" Bronwyn was exasperated and she got off the bed and walked to the window. "And will it be easier for you? No, you'll just pine for him. The only person who would benefit from that would be your fucking mother! Oh, she'd love that. She'd have won, don't you see?"

"I don't want to talk about her. I can't even begin to think about *her*," replied Rosina. "I feel sorry for her anyway, having to give birth to me, keeping me and looking at me every day, reminding her…"

Bronwyn turned and slammed her hands against the window in frustration. There was going to be no getting through to Rosina, she could see that now. And for someone like Bronwyn, who was used to always getting what she wanted, it was incredibly infuriating to be unable to get Rosina to see that none of this was her fault.

Connor, still sitting on the doorstep, jumped when he heard someone hit the window upstairs. He hauled himself up and hobbled to the curb to look up at the window. He saw Bronwyn, palms flat against the window, a look of angry frustration on her face. Taking advantage of the fact that she didn't know he was there, he stood and watched her until he felt in a strange way like he was intruding, and then hobbled back to the step.

Ten minutes later, she came out of the house and stood in front of him on the step.

"I can't get through to her," she said. "She won't listen to me."

He managed a wan smile.

"I find it hard to believe there's someone who doesn't listen to you."

"Me too, it doesn't happen often." She shifted from foot to foot. "I've taken care of her all our lives. I've sorted out anyone who's hurt her, and I've protected her from her mother. This, though, it feels hopeless." She sighed and shook her head. "I'll come back tomorrow, is that okay?"

"Yes, please come. I'm sure if we work together we can get her to see that none of this is her fault. It's her bloody mother. Someone should have a word with that woman," replied Connor.

Bronwyn narrowed her eyes and a look of anger crossed her face.

"Don't worry," she said to Connor as she walked out of the gate. "You leave that bitch to me."

As Bronwyn walked down the street, Connor couldn't help pondering her words. Strange, Bronwyn had almost repeated what his mother had said the night before, about being there to protect Rosina. Was that how he felt too?

* * * *

When she heard someone knock on her door, Kathleen's head snapped up and she turned towards it.

"Rosina?" she asked and took no notice when she banged the table in her haste to get to the door, knocking over the four empty wine bottles.

When she flung open the door, she was confused to see Bronwyn standing on her doorstep.

"Look—" she began but was cut off by Bronwyn leaping up the step towards her.

In her drunken haze she couldn't dodge Bronwyn's fist. As it smashed into her face, she staggered and fell back into the hall.

"You bitch!" Bronwyn came into the hall, kicking the door closed behind her.

Kathleen looked up, stunned, and paid no heed to her throbbing eye. A red haze came over her and instead of her daughter's best friend standing before her, she saw *him*, Rosina's father, and let out a wail as she lurched towards Bronwyn. They wrestled together but Bronwyn was stronger and pushed Kathleen back to the floor where she crouched down in front of her.

"Leave Rosina alone. Never, ever, see her again, you poisonous *bitch*!" spat Bronwyn.

"She's my girl—my baby," Kathleen screamed back in Bronwyn's face and collapsed in a weeping heap on the floor.

Bronwyn stared with a mixture of hate and pity as Kathleen curled herself into a fetal position and sobbed.

"She's nothing to you," replied Bronwyn and, leaving Kathleen where she was, quietly let herself out of the house.

* * * *

Barry turned up for his cell meeting, full of good intentions that tonight he was going to tell Andy that it was his last night as an I.R.A member. He was the first to arrive and he followed Andy through to the kitchen.

"Listen, Andy, I need to speak to you before the others get here," He took the can of beer that Andy gave him.

Andy, a thin, red haired man with piercing blue eyes, nodded and gestured for Barry to sit down.

"This isn't for me, being a member here. I can't take the strain of it anymore," the words that Barry had rehearsed over and over came out easily and he relaxed a little.

Andy regarded Barry with a serious expression before he pulled out a chair and sat opposite.

"You're a good man, Barry, a decent sort, and you know we don't keep anyone here against their will."

Barry sagged with relief and took a sip of his beer.

"Can I ask you something, Baz, now you're no longer involved?"

"Sure."

"A lot of jobs have been getting messed up recently. Do you think we've got an informer in this cell?"

Barry froze, the can of beer halfway to his mouth as he raised his eyes to meet Andy's. As he stared into those empty blue eyes, Barry knew, right at that moment, that Andy was aware of everything. He recovered quickly and put the beer back on the table.

"I've never suspected anybody," he said. "Do you really believe that we've a mole here?"

"Hey, don't listen to me. I'm just a natural paranoid I guess." Andy reached across the table and held his hand out. "It's been good knowing you, Barry."

Was it just Barry's mistrustful and confused state of mind, or were Andy's last words loaded with a threatening warning?

Barry shook Andy's hand and stood up, wanting to get out of the house as quickly as possible now. As he left the house, he knew that was it.

Game over.

He walked briskly home in a mild state of shock. Andy *knew*! How long had he known, and what was he planning to do? Barry was well versed in the ways of the I.R.A. He had been given extensive lectures on what was likely to happen if a member ever found out that he was undercover. It meant death, and if by any chance Barry got away from Crossmaglen, indeed out of Northern Ireland altogether, he would spend the rest of his life in hiding, with a new name, a new identity, and no contact with his family.

But as he walked, Barry couldn't even think that far into the future. His first priority was to run, as far as he could and as fast as possible.

Stopping at a phone box, he glanced around to make sure he wasn't being watched and picked up the telephone to ring Johnny. It was now up to Johnny to make the necessary arrangements to get him out of here alive and in one piece.

Before he dialed the number in full he suddenly hung up the telephone and stared out into the street. A thought had occurred to him; what if Johnny had set him up? Maybe Johnny was so pissed at him quitting as an agent he had spilled the beans to Andy?

"Shit," Barry whispered and leaned his head against the side of the phone booth.

Suddenly feeling very confused and vulnerable, Barry pushed open the door and stumbled back into the street and straight into the arms of Andy.

Barry shrieked and pushed at the man's chest.

"Hey, man, it's only me!" Andy slapped him on the back. "You want to watch where you're going!"

Andy's face was friendly enough, but Barry didn't buy it. He wondered for a second if this was it, if this was his time to die, and before he could find out, he turned tail and fled, not stopping until he reached home.

* * * *

Barry crashed through the front door only moments after Bronwyn arrived home. Bronwyn was part way through telling Alia about Rosina's sorry state when Barry half fell into the kitchen. He was wheezing, desperately trying to catch his breath, and he leaned over and clutched at his chest.

"I need to get out of here. I have to leave, Mam!" Barry pulled himself up and gripped Alia's arms. "Mam, I'm really fucking scared!"

Alia stared at Barry in horror. Of her two children, Barry was the one who was always calm, never in a flap or a crisis. Now, as she looked at the wild-eyed boy in front of her, she barely recognised him.

"Barry…" Tentatively, Bronwyn touched his arm. "What have you done?"

Barry moaned and let go of Alia. He spun around and clutched at his head.

"I can't tell you but, oh God, I need you to help me!" he cried and his voice got higher and higher until he was almost screaming at his mother and sister. "You need to help me! Hide me! I have to get away!"

Bronwyn stepped forward and slapped his face hard. He stopped his rant and turned to her with large eyes.

"Are you one of them?" he asked and cowered back into the hall.

"Barry!" Alia shouted and he jumped.

"It's me, just your ma and Bronwyn. Barry, please, you're scaring us…" Alia was weeping now and Bronwyn clung onto her mother's arm.

As Barry stared at his mother, the fog started to clear in his head and he took a deep breath and held his hand up.

"A minute, just gimme a minute." He got his breathing steady again and nodded to himself.

"Barry, come and sit down," Bronwyn implored and when he looked at her now he knew that it was she, just his sister, Bronwyn, and not one of the crazy demons that, in his moments of clarity, he could see haunting him.

Eventually he returned to the kitchen and sat down.

"Sorry," he mumbled.

"Tell us what's going on." Bronwyn took his hand and spoke in soothing tones. "You've been acting weird for ages, Barry, and if you tell us we might be able to help you."

"I'm ill," he said. "Voices, in my head or, maybe, they're not, I don't know…" his words made no sense and Bronwyn exchanged a worried glance with her mother.

"And…and I can't sleep! I keep hearing voices in my head and people are watching me—everywhere I go they're stalking me!" Barry's voice rose in panic again and this time neither Bronwyn nor Alia could placate him.

"Oh, it's starting again!" Barry grabbed his head and stood up, knocking his chair over. "Make it stop! Please, stop them—make them stop!" He ended his tirade with a roar. Then he spun around and swept the plates that Alia had laid out for dinner off the table.

Bronwyn and Alia leapt out of their seats and clutched at each other, frightened of this new Barry that they had never seen before.

Barry didn't stop. He crashed around the kitchen, bouncing off the units and cupboards, punching the walls, picking up and hurling anything that got in his way. A stray china plate caught Bronwyn on her forehead and she fell back, screaming when she felt the blood that trickled down her face.

"I'm calling the police!" Alia shrieked and ran into the hall, dragging Bronwyn along behind her.

Once there, they slammed the door on Barry and Alia fumbled for the telephone.

As Alia sobbed out their predicament to the emergency services operator, Bronwyn realised that there was silence from the other side of the door. She opened it a crack and peered through to see Barry sitting amongst the mess of broken crockery and mugs and bottles.

"Barry?" she whispered.

He turned towards her and her mouth fell open at the sight of him.

He sat cross-legged on the floor, tears streaming down his face, and blood streaming down his arms.

"Sorry, Bronwyn," he whispered in reply, dropping the shard of china he had used to slash his wrists.

* * * *

Everything happened very quickly after that. Bronwyn skittered back down the hall and grabbed the phone out of Alia's hand.

"Make that an ambulance," she told the operator. "My brother's slit his wrists. Please, send it as soon as possible."

With that she handed the phone back to a stunned Alia and ran back into the kitchen, grabbing a tea towel on her way. She fell to her knees beside Barry and grabbed his left arm. Working quickly she wrapped the towel as tight as she could around his bleeding arm, talking to him all the time in a hushed voice.

"You're gonna be fine, Barry. We'll get you some help, and we can deal with it, right?" She glanced up at him.

Barry stared back through half closed eyes and she panicked and shouted in his ear.

"Barry!"

He snapped his head up and looked at her, dazed and confused.

"There we go, you stay with me now."

Bronwyn called to Alia when she heard her hang up the phone.

"Ma, more towels, or bandages, or something."

Alia reacted well, considering the sight that met her eyes when she came back into the kitchen. Blood, puddles of it, was now gathering around Barry and she clapped her hand to her mouth when she saw the pallor of his skin.

"Towels, ma," Bronwyn said. Alia nodded and, scooping up fresh ones from the laundry basket, she brought them over.

With both arms tied and Barry looking almost comatose, there was nothing else for Bronwyn to do to help her brother. She couldn't stand it, being useless, so she told Alia to stay with him and she went out front to wait for the ambulance.

As she stood in the street, with the wind howling around her and snow starting to fall again, she glanced back towards the house, then up into the sky.

"God, if you're there, you better bloody help us now."

* * * *

News spread quickly in the small town of Crossmaglen, and details, some true, some false, of Barry's breakdown traveled through the grapevine.

Danny heard one of the false versions, as he took his breakfast in the Fox and Hound. It was Lila, the landlady, who told Danny how Barry had gone insane, smashing up the house before attacking his mother and sister.

Danny's first thought was of Bronwyn. He left the pub and immediately made his way to the hospital.

When he arrived at accident and emergency, he spotted Bronwyn at the coffee machine and ran up to her.

She was not surprised to see him; after all he was one of Barry's best friends.

"How is he? How are you?" He took in the stitches on her forehead and tried not to look at the black eye that he had caused.

"I'm fine, getting used to being wounded," she said dryly.

There was an uncomfortable silence and he had the decency to flush a dark shade of red.

"Sorry, that was uncalled for," she said, looking around. The last thing she needed now was for her mother to see Danny here.

"Let's go outside, I need some air."

They walked out and sat on the wall in the ambulance-parking bay.

"What happened?" Danny asked. "I've heard a couple of stories and I don't know what's true."

"I don't know what's wrong with him—he just went mad. But he's been acting weird for a while now. The doctors said something about stress…"

"Baz had nothing to be stressed about, he was fine!" Danny exclaimed.

"It's one of those things," said Bronwyn.

"I'm sorry for what happened—I mean—what I done to you," said Danny. "You didn't deserve that."

"Yeah, well, lucky that the cavalry arrived," she replied.

"Who was that guy?" asked Danny. "He could have broken my nose."

"He was a guy from the barracks, Stu, his name was."

Danny felt a slow burn of anger and his tone changed.

"Stu, huh? He the guy you dumped me for?"

"Jesus, Danny, I didn't know him before that night, and if he hadn't been there you might have killed me!" she exclaimed.

"Don't be so fucking dramatic! So, how many times have you seen him?" Danny asked roughly.

"Twice!" she said. "And if I want, I'll see him again."

Danny laughed and shook his head. "You're a soldier doll. This past year I've been with you, and all the time you're running after a fucking soldier. I guess you live up to your reputation, hey?"

"What reputation?" Bronwyn was indignant.

"For being a slag! The tough girl about town, Bronwyn Ranger, she'll be anybody's for a pint!"

Danny's words cut deep and Bronwyn was devastated, but she would rather die than let Danny see that he had hurt her.

Before she could reply, Danny jumped off the wall.

"Give Baz my best, I'll see him soon." As he muttered the short sentence he glanced over her shoulder. As Danny jogged away, she turned around to see Connor making his way over to her. She uttered a laugh. Danny was so scared of Connor, now he would do anything to stay out of his way.

"Was he bothering you?" Connor asked when he reached her. "Jesus, what happened to your face?"

"You asked me that yesterday," said Bronwyn.

He reached out and touched her face, next to the fresh stitches and her skin tingled at his touch.

"This wasn't here yesterday. Did that bastard hit you again?"

"No, it was an accident with a plate," she said and moved away from him. "What are you doing here?"

"My stitches burst." He pulled up his trouser leg and showed her his bullet wound.

A couple of the stitches had torn and it was bleeding.

"God, we're all in the wars lately. How's Rosie?"

Connor's face fell and he shrugged.

"She wasn't up when I left. I'm going to try to get her to come out to dinner tonight, take her mind off things. Anyway, are you going home now? If not, do you have time for a coffee while I wait to get this seen to?"

"I'm not going home yet. I've been here all night. My brother's in there." She nodded to the hospital.

"Is he okay?" Connor asked.

"Not really." Tears sprang to her eyes and she turned away. "He's in a right fucking mess and I can't help him."

Connor laid his hand on her shoulder. She let out a cry and turned into his comforting embrace. He held her there and she wrapped her arms around him, shaking with silent sobs.

"Want to tell me about it?" he asked quietly, and she nodded into his chest.

But she didn't want to tell him, not quite yet. She liked it where she was, breathing in the smell of him and liking the feel of his strong arms around her. The last few days had been a turmoil of emotions for Bronwyn, what with Rosina and Danny, along with Connor making her feel things she shouldn't be feeling, and now Barry. So she clung onto Connor, pretending for a while that she was in the right place, with the right man, until all she could see in her mind's eye was Rosina's hurt and angry face and she pulled away.

"Sorry," she mumbled.

He took her hand and led her back inside the hospital, where he found a quiet corner and sat her down on one of the hard-backed chairs.

"Tell me what's going on with your brother," he said, sitting down next to her.

She told him everything, not only about Barry, but also about her fears for Rosina, her troubles with Danny, and her visit to Kathleen the day before. The only thing she didn't confide in Connor was her mixed feelings for him.

"You punched Rosina's mother?" Connor stared at her in shock. "Seriously?"

"Yeah." Bronwyn hung her head. "I'm a hothead. I can't help it, and I'm a bit ashamed, but she hurt Rosie so bad. I couldn't *not* do anything."

"You love Rosina very much, don't you?" he asked.

She nodded and smiled through her tears. "She's my best friend."

And that's why you'll never know what I'm feeling for you.

Chapter Twelve

Drama at the Camp

"Are you okay?" Connor asked.

They were in the Italian restaurant that they had been to on Christmas Eve and Rosina was lost in her own thoughts.

"Yeah, I'm okay," she said, but Connor knew different.

It had taken a lot of work for him to get her out of bed, let alone out of the house, and now that they were here he was determined to make sure she enjoyed the night out.

"Was your meal all right?"

She had left half of the main course on her plate.

"It was lovely, I'm just not too hungry," she replied.

"Can you manage a cherry pie? I promise there'll be nothing but cherries in it tonight."

His comment raised a half hearted smile from her and sighing, Connor leaned back in his chair and thought back to the last time they were here, how happy they had been that night. He wished that she could be that happy again, but watching her transformation since the revelations about her father, he didn't think it was possible. Since her mother had broken the news to her about her father, there had been a black cloud hanging over her and nothing he or anyone else did or said seemed to be able to shake it off.

"Maybe we can skip dessert, take a walk home?" she asked.

"It's a long walk," he said doubtfully. "How about we get a taxi to the Fox and Hound, stop in and see if Bronwyn's working, then walk from there?"

"Yes, that would be fine," she replied.

Connor sighed. A week ago she would have panicked at the thought of Connor being seen on the wrong side of the divide, but, when he had mentioned going to the Fox and Hound just now, the danger he might face hadn't even occurred to her. He stood up and left the money for the bill on the table.

"Ready?" He held out his hand and she took it.

"Ready," she said and together they left the restaurant.

When the taxi dropped them off at the Fox and Hound, she clutched his hand as they walked to the door.

"Are you sure you want to be here? People are not going to be very friendly."

"Don't worry, we won't be staying that long. If Bronwyn's not here we'll leave."

When they entered the pub nobody gave them a second glance. They pushed through the crowds to the bar and Connor was pleased to see that Bronwyn was on duty.

"Hey!" he called and she saw him and waved.

"With you in a minute!" she called and finished serving.

"Rosie!" she exclaimed when she came over to him. "Good to see you, babe."

"You too, Bron." Rosina glanced nervously around her.

"Hey, I'm leaving now. Want to come through the back while I get my things?"

They followed her through and when they sat down in the back room Rosina asked how Barry was.

"They were doing tests when I left. I'm going back to the hospital to see if they've got any closer to finding out what's wrong with him."

"Poor Barry," murmured Rosina.

"I know, but he'll be fine, I'm sure," replied Bronwyn. "But, Rosie, how are you?"

Rosina shrugged and Bronwyn looked at Connor. He shook his head and Bronwyn frowned and turned her attention back to Rosina.

"You'll be fine. You've got us, and we're all you need, okay?" Bronwyn stood up. "I should get back to the hospital. I'll walk with you guys."

As Rosina walked ahead of them, Bronwyn caught Connor's arm and pulled him back.

"She's not looking good, Connor," she said with a worried expression.

Connor stopped and turned to Bronwyn.

"I know, and I don't know what else I can do."

Just two miles down the road from the Fox and Hound, Stu looked out over the grounds of the camp. The barracks were almost deserted. The majority of soldiers had been called out to a problem in nearby Carrickmacross, where the towns own supply of army soldiers were stretched to the limit after an attack on the local government offices. Stu, Carter, and another corporal called Lee were the only men left on the camp. They were all sitting in the observation tower, drinking the Irish liqueur that Bronwyn had given Stu on Christmas Day.

"Better not get any trouble tonight. Three of us can't handle any bother from the locals," said Lee as he glanced at the computer screens.

"It's been quiet for the last week. We'll be okay." Stu pulled a pack of cards from his pocket and held them up. "Who's up for a game of poker?"

The three men played awhile until the snow began to fall heavily and Lee got up to close the hatch against the whistling wind.

"Shit!" he said as he passed the computer desk.

"What?" Stu and Carter turned around and looked over his shoulder at the monitor.

What they saw made Stu's blood run cold. A dozen or so men were at the gates of the camp, and, upon closer inspection, it looked like they were planting some device in the ground to try to blow up the gates to gain access to the grounds.

"Oh fuck, we didn't set the alarms!" said Stu in horror.

"Carter, you help me get us armed. Stu, call up Carrickmacross and tell them we need our fucking men back!" With that Lee grabbed Carter's arm and pulled him through the hatch.

Stu dialed up the neighbouring army base and requested emergency assistance. That job done, with shaking hands he unlocked the cupboard that contained their weapons and pulled out four rifles and enough ammunition to blow up half of Crossmaglen. He ran full speed to the window that looked out over the gates and clipped the telephoto lens onto the rifle. Trying to keep it steady, he opened the window and settled the rifle on the ledge. Looking through the lens, he finally got it in focus and tensed himself, ready for action.

* * * *

Bronwyn, Connor, and Rosina had just turned the corner in the lane that ran parallel to the army base when the gates exploded. The blast of the detonation startled them. Connor grabbed Bronwyn and Rosina and pulled them to the ground. Debris flew through the night sky and landed around them. They lay in the snow until the sky had stopped hailing pieces of metal and earth upon them.

"Holy shit!" Bronwyn sat up and looked over to the base. It was now crawling with men and, as a burst of machine gun fire sounded from inside the camp, Bronwyn leapt to her feet.

"Get down!" yelled Connor as he pulled Rosina into the woods that lined the road.

"Stu!" Bronwyn whispered. Without stopping to think about the consequences should she get caught, she ran towards the army base.

By the time Connor realised that Bronwyn wasn't on the lane, he could no longer see her through the heavy snow that was falling. He ran back into the woods and sat next to Rosina.

"You stay here, do you understand?" He clasped her shoulders. "You stay down, and don't come out until I get back, okay?"

"Don't go!" she cried and grabbed his hand.

"I'll be right back," he replied and pulled his hand away.

With that he stumbled back out of the woods and onto the lane. Checking that it was clear, he ran as well as his injured leg would allow and made it across the other side of the road to the fence of the army base. Kneeling down, he peered through the fence. There were men, identifiable as being I.R.A by their ski masks. He tried to count but they were crawling all over the camp; there could have been eight, maybe more. He spotted four bodies lying near the fence in the snow and his heart lurched at the thought that one of them could be Bronwyn. He edged closer and although he couldn't see clearly, he was pretty certain that they were all men.

What the hell had made Bronwyn bolt like she had? Had she recognised one of these guys as Danny? Suddenly one of the men walked right in front of Connor on the other side of the fence, and he held his breath as a Thompson sub-machine gun dangled in front of his face. The man moved on and

Connor breathed again before crawling round the fence towards the rear of the camp.

When the gates blew, Stu was ready and as the men poured through the smoke he opened fire. Two went down, but another seven or eight flooded through the broken gates and into the camp.

He heard a blast of machine gun fire from the barracks and he whooped in delight as another man got caught in the blast. They split up then, six that Stu could see clearly and a group of four men. He had his rifle trained on the men who sprinted in the direction of the Northeast Sanger. He followed them with the lens of the rifle, trigger finger ready, when he noticed that as they ran they were dropping something after them.

POW!

Explosives. They must have loads of them! What if they tried to blow up the tower?

"Shit!" he muttered and let off the rest of the rounds in the rifle.

When it was spent he reloaded. Reaching out, he flicked on the beam that bathed the campground in light.

Connor threw himself down on the ground when the light came on. He glanced around and panicked when he realised he was practically out in the open. He crawled forward, heading for the side of the camp where the grass grew tall and thick. He had nearly made it when a shot whizzed past his ear. He lay flat on the ground, breathing heavily and trying to flatten himself into the snow. The soldiers were shooting at him! They thought he was one of *them;* he could hardly stand up and wave a white flag or the I.R.A men would pelt him with bullets. When no further shots were fired, he pushed his hands into the snow and pulled himself into the grass where he lay on his back, trying to ignore the pain in his leg.

Bronwyn ran around the edge of the camp and threw herself to the ground as another bomb exploded just feet away. She looked up when the smoke had cleared and saw the bomb had blasted the back fence away. Two men lay amongst the mangled fence, their faces bloodied, and she averted her eyes from the corpses. She pulled herself to her hands and knees and, crawling into the camp, she made her way over to the barracks where she hunched down in the shadows of the building. As she began to wonder what had possessed her to run in here and get stuck in the middle of a deadly battle, two men suddenly came hurtling out of the barracks and ran past her towards the tower on the other side of the camp.

Bronwyn curled herself into a ball and sat with her head in her arms.

Stu swung around with the rifle as someone came through the hatch. He only just managed to stop his finger pulling the trigger as Carter and Lee hauled themselves up and into the tower.

"We got about seven, I think," Lee gasped as he tried to catch his breath after the sprint across camp. "There's maybe another three running around out there."

Stu nodded and turned back to the window. He caught sight of two people making their way across the edge of the camp near one of the barracks and he aimed and fired. He got one, and the other guy looked at his companion, who was writhing on the ground, and darted into the barracks.

"Gotcha!" whispered Stu. Throwing the rifle aside, he grabbed Carter's machine gun and made for the hatch.

"Hey!" Carter said, following Stu. "Where are you going? We should stay up here until reinforcements get here."

"Cover me," called Stu as he lowered himself down, landing in the snow.

Moving quickly, he ran across to the barracks and fell to his knees next to the man that he had shot. Keeping very quiet, he raised his head and looked through the window. There was one of them in there, and Stu's blood boiled as he realised the man was emptying their supplies of weapons, stowing them into two large black bags. He checked that Carter's gun was loaded and, taking a deep breath, he crashed through the door, aiming the machine gun.

The man spun around, his own hands loaded with weapons, and for a second they stood still, neither making the first move.

"Drop the shit!" yelled Stu, taking a step towards the man.

Just outside, Bronwyn sat up when she heard Stu shout from inside the building. She crawled over to the window and pulled herself up from the ground. Peering through the window she saw Stu standing by the open door on the opposite side of the building. She glanced to her left and when she recognised Danny as the man standing with an armful of weapons, she sank back down into the snow.

Shit!

What was Danny doing here?

Bronwyn rose up and looked through the window again. The situation inside hadn't changed; Stu stood with his legs apart, the gun in his hands aimed at Danny. Danny stood still, looking down at all of the guns he held and Bronwyn knew he was trying to work out which ones might be loaded. Danny would shoot Stu, she knew he was capable, and she knew that Danny would shoot to kill.

There was only one way to stop him, and that was if she got in the way. Danny would never shoot her, she was sure of it.

Bronwyn broke into a run and as she rounded the corner of the building she could hear Danny and Stu shouting at each other. She tripped over the dead man and skidded through the door, landing at Stu's feet. Gasping, she grabbed Stu's arm and pulled herself up to stand in front of him.

"Drop it, Danny. I won't let you do this," she said.

Danny stared at her in astonishment and he didn't even notice when the pile of guns fell from his arms to the floor.

"What the fuck?" he said. "Why are you here? Get the fuck out!"

She shook her head and stood her ground.

"If I have to go through you to get to him, I will," Danny said softly.

"Bullshit," replied Bronwyn.

Stu grabbed Bronwyn and in one fluid motion he pulled her to his side. She struggled and wrenched her arm away from him.

In the seconds that their brief struggle took, Danny stooped and picked up one of the shotguns that lay at his feet. Stu, still trying to drag Bronwyn towards the door, heard the click of the safety catch and he turned, with Bronwyn still in his grip. It all happened quickly, but to Bronwyn it seemed like she was in a slow motion movie. Danny raised the gun, and both Bronwyn and Stu realised that she would take that bullet if Danny pulled the trigger.

"Danny, no!" Bronwyn screamed, covering her face.

Simultaneously pushing Bronwyn aside and raising his machine gun, Stu let off four quick bursts of fire. A single shot fired from Danny's shotgun, and then there was silence.

Connor heard Bronwyn scream and he sat bolt upright as the barracks lit up with machine gun fire.

This time he ran with all his might, slamming down onto his injured leg, the pain only spurring him on to reach her. He ran through the same hole in the fence that Bronwyn had used to gain access to the camp, and as he reached the barracks, he ran through the open door, not caring that there could still be a gunman in there. The room was smoky, but he could make out Bronwyn's inert body lying on the ground.

"Bronwyn!" he shouted. Running to her, he fell to his knees and hauled her up to face him.

She opened her eyes, stared into his, and he yelled with joy that she wasn't hurt. Before he could ask if she was okay, he was grabbed by his shirt and pulled out of her reach across the floor. Suddenly he found himself staring at the wrong end of a machine gun. He held his hands up and looked towards Bronwyn. She crawled across the floor and, reaching up, moved the gun away.

"It's okay, Stu. He's with me," she said in a shaky voice and stood up.

She walked across the room and stared down at the ruin that used to be her boyfriend. Danny was lying on his stomach, blood pooling around his body. Bronwyn grabbed his jacket and heaved him towards her until he was lying on his back. His eyes were open, and his chest heaved in a jagged fashion with every dying breath that he took.

"Oh, God," she whispered.

He locked his eyes on hers and each time he breathed out, droplets of blood sprayed from his mouth.

Quickly, Bronwyn unzipped his jacket and roughly pulled up his shirt. His body was riddled with bullets. She pulled the shirt back down, knowing that there was nothing she could do to save him now. She took his hand and held it tight, tears dripping from her face onto him. A few seconds later, his eyes rolled back and his chest stopped its rise and fall.

"Get out," said Stu eventually. "You two, get out now."

Connor understood; although Danny was dead, there were surely more of his kind around the base, and they were still in danger. He limped over to Bronwyn, pulling her away from Danny.

"Come on, sweetheart, come with me," he said softly and, with a last glance back, she allowed herself to be led away.

Holding hands, they ran around the edge of the barracks until they came to the place where the fence was missing. Bronwyn stopped and looked back at the camp.

"Danny…" she whispered.

Connor pulled her out of the camp, back towards the woods where he hoped to God Rosina was still hiding. It would be all he needed for her to go missing now. He realised that Bronwyn was still babbling and he clapped a hand to her mouth.

"Shh, we need to stay quiet. We don't know how many more of them are around."

She nodded and he took his hand away.

"He would have shot me!" she whispered to Connor. "Danny was going to shoot me." Her eyes filled with tears and Connor pulled her down into the thick grass where he had originally hidden. He pulled her close to him.

"But he didn't," he said. "You're here, alive—safe now— as long as we get home as soon as possible."

She pulled away and looked up into his face. A slight frown knitted her brow and she put her hand up to touch his face. His eyes gleamed very bright in the moonlight.

"You came after me," she stated.

"Yes," he replied.

For a moment it didn't seem to matter that they were in the middle of a war zone, or that Danny was dead and Rosina lay somewhere nearby waiting patiently to be rescued. All that Bronwyn could think about was that she was here, with Connor, and all she had to do was lean forward and touch his sweet lips with her own and it would all be over; he would know then how she felt, and she wouldn't have to lie to herself anymore…

"Bronwyn?" Rosina's voice came out of the darkness and they pulled apart like the guilty lovers that they very nearly were.

"Connor, oh, thank God." She was crawling through the grass behind them and, when she reached them, she sat down heavily in the snow.

"Rosie, are you all right?" whispered Bronwyn.

"Yeah, I got scared. You were both gone so long."

Bronwyn saw Connor's guilty expression and felt her face flush.

"Are you okay, Bron? I heard someone scream." Rosina put her hand on Bronwyn's arm.

"Danny's dead," she said, looking back towards the camp.

Connor took both girls by their arms and stood up, pulling them with him.

"And so will we be, if we don't get out of here," he said and they quietly made their way back to the lane.

Rosina held Bronwyn's arm as they hurried into the woods. Connor was quite far behind them, as he struggled along with his injured leg, when he heard a shout behind him. He turned and his eyes widened as he saw the man dressed in black standing only yards away. The man had no mask on and realised too late he could now be identified. He didn't hesitate as he raised his rifle and aimed it at Connor.

The first shot went wide and Connor didn't stop to see if his luck would hold. He bolted over the hill that led down to the lane, trying to keep low, as he heard the sound of the man reloading his rifle behind him. He could hear Rosina screaming his name and, as he reached the brow of the hill, saw her running out into the lane, Bronwyn holding on to her arm to try to pull her back to safety.

"Get back!" he yelled at them. As another bullet whizzed past his head, he lost his footing and went down, tumbling over and over, eventually landing in the bushes at the far side of the road.

He screamed as he felt a searing pain in his leg, then pushed his face into the snow to stop himself yelling. After a moment he pulled himself together, knowing if he stayed there it would be the end of all three of them.

Bronwyn and Rosina crashed through the bushes as he was getting to his feet. Bronwyn reached him first and when she saw the fresh blood that stained the snow she thought he had been shot again. She pulled him up and slung his arm over her shoulder.

"Come on, Rosie, get his other arm," she instructed.

Between the two of them, they managed to move further into the woods and away from the shots that were still being fired intermittently.

They went straight to Bronwyn's. As she opened the door and they piled in, she realised that the house was in darkness; her mother must still be at the hospital.

"Let me see your leg," she said to Connor, as they helped him into the lounge.

He pulled up his trouser leg and the two girls knelt at his feet to examine it.

"Rosie, can you get me some water, something to stop it bleeding?" Bronwyn asked. Rosina ran off to the kitchen.

"It's fine," said Connor through gritted teeth, then yelped as Bronwyn touched the wound.

"I thought you'd been shot again," she said. "But it's just the stitches. You scraped it all up and made it bleed again."

Rosina came back into the room with a jug of water and a strip of white cloth.

"I tore up a pillowcase, I hope it's okay," she said anxiously as she passed it over to Bronwyn.

"It's fine." Bronwyn stood up. "Can you do this, Rosie? I really need to phone the hospital and find out how Barry is."

As Bronwyn stood in the hall and glanced back at Connor, she found it hard to believe what she had come close to doing on that hillside. Connor belonged with Rosina, and Rosina was her best friend. She had to put thoughts of him out of her mind, because she wouldn't hurt Rosina for any man.

Connor looked up at Bronwyn while she was talking on the telephone. Something had sparked between them back at the army base, and it hadn't been the first time. But he loved Rosina with all his heart, and she needed him more than ever now.

"Is this okay?" Rosina looked up at him and he smiled and touched her face.

"It's fine, Rosie." He glanced down at the makeshift bandage. "You did a real good job."

* * * *

"What the fuck happened?"

Jason Brady, cell leader of Danny's division of the I.R.A, stood and looked around at the three faces in front of him. They were bruised and bloodied, their clothing torn, and they said nothing, just stared back at him.

"Twelve men went into that camp. There were only three soldiers there and it should have been a piece of piss to take them out and unload their weapons. Now, here we are, with none of them dead, yet only three of you come back alive with *no weapons*!"

Mickey, the man who had seen Connor and had shot at him, spoke up.

"They weren't alone. Someone else was there with them. He wasn't one of ours but he wasn't military either. I think he was a Protestant."

Jason leaned in close to Mickey and tilted his head to one side.

"Now, what makes you think that?"

"I think I recognised him. I'm pretty sure it was the lad we jumped a couple of weeks ago. Connor something, the one who was seeing that Rosina James."

Jason sat back and simmered in his anger. The job had been planned for weeks, and it should have been so easy. He had gone so far as to arrange the attack on the barracks at Carrickmacross, and an insider he had stationed there had called the majority of the Crossmaglen soldiers out of the town. Three left; three bullets was all it should have taken, and they would have had their arms supplied for a year or more. But by chance, or an unlucky coincidence, that damn Prod had got in the way, and now more than half of his cell was dead. Jason stood up and directed his next words to Mickey.

"Find him. Kill him."

* * * *

Bronwyn came back into the room and slumped down on the settee next to Connor.

"Barry's had a nervous breakdown. It's been confirmed," she said.

"Jesus, will he be okay?" asked Connor.

Bronwyn's eyes filled with tears and she wiped them angrily away.

"They're taking him to Banbridge."

She didn't have to say anymore for both Connor and Rosina knew what she meant. Banbridge was a small town about forty miles north of Crossmaglen and it held the largest mental institute in Northern Ireland. It had a fearsome reputation; only the most severe cases went to Banbridge. Normally, if you were sent there, you didn't come back.

"Hold on, you don't get sent to Banbridge for a nervous breakdown," said Connor.

"There might be more," she said quietly. "They're doing other psychiatric tests as well."

Rosina stood up and hugged Bronwyn. "He'll be okay, you'll see," she said. "Do you want me to stay?"

"No, I'll be fine," Bronwyn said and looked at Connor. "Make sure you get that leg looked at properly tomorrow."

"I will, don't worry," he said and led Rosina out of the door. "See ya."

When she closed the door behind them, Bronwyn sat on the bottom stair in the hallway. God, it was all too much to take. Barry's mental breakdown, Danny's death, Stu saving her from getting shot, with Connor and her feelings for him thrown in as an extra measure, she felt completely exhausted. Not bothering to turn off the light in the lounge, Bronwyn made her way upstairs and flopped down on the bed. There was so much to think about, but she felt utterly wretched. Before she could even begin to contemplate all that had happened, she fell fast asleep.

* * * *

When Alia came home a little after midnight she went into the lounge, expecting Bronwyn to be waiting for her. When she saw the jug of water and the blood soaked towel, she panicked and ran up the stairs to Bronwyn's room.

She saw Bronwyn lying, fully clothed, on her bed and she leapt into the room and stared down at her daughter. Was she hurt? She didn't look like it, or maybe she was unconscious?

The thought snapped her into action and she grabbed Bronwyn and shook her, calling her name at the same time.

"What? What? Ma?" Bronwyn sat up and gripped Alia's arms. "Is it Barry?"

"Oh, God." Alia sank down onto the bed and pulled Bronwyn close to her. "I thought you were hurt, my baby." She stroked her daughter's hair and Bronwyn took comfort in her mother's arms.

"I'm fine," she said.

"But there's blood downstairs, lots of it," Alia said.

"Oh, that was Connor. Listen, I should tell you what went down tonight, but I want to know about Barry as well. Shall we go downstairs?"

In the early hours of the morning of the 27th December, Alia and Bronwyn sat at the kitchen table where they had enjoyed many a mother/daughter chat, and Bronwyn told her mother the tale of the events of the night that had nearly got her killed.

Alia listened in horror to the story and when Bronwyn told her that Danny had been shot dead, she began to look frightened.

"Did they know you were there? Because they'll come after you," she said.

Bronwyn shook her head.

"Nobody knew, only Stu and Danny. Stu won't say anything because I shouldn't have been on the campgrounds and he'd get it in the neck. He's not like that anyway, he's kind of…special." She shook her head and wondered why she had chosen those words to describe Stu, a man she barely knew. "And Danny won't say anything, he can't…"

An unexpected lump came to Bronwyn's throat as she remembered Danny how he used to be, when they were kids, before the I.R.A had taken over his life.

"I'm so sorry about Dan. It could have been so different for him," said Alia. "What a wasted life."

"I know, and Connor nearly got killed as well. Just as we were leaving, one of Danny's lot spotted him and opened fire. He was lucky," Bronwyn said.

"Good Christ!" Alia widened her eyes. "Did they know him? Would the man be able to recognise him again? Because, if so, Connor's as good as dead already."

Bronwyn put her head in her hands and groaned. She knew it was true; in this sort of situation, Connor would be hunted down and shot before he had the chance to talk to anyone. Damn it!

"I should warn him," she said and scraped back her chair.

"Bronwyn, please, *please*, don't get any more involved than you are," Alia begged as Bronwyn made for the telephone.

Bronwyn's hand wavered for a second as she reached for the phone. Then she picked it up and turned toward her mother.

"Ma, it's Connor. He's been real good to me and to Rosina. I can't not warn him."

Alia waved her hand in submission; she knew that Bronwyn was too much of a good person not to get involved. It was a big part of why she loved her so. It could also be the reason that she might end up getting herself killed.

Once Bronwyn had finished the call to Connor, she came back into the kitchen.

"He had thought of it already. He's going to try and get Rosie to go away with him for a bit," she told Alia.

"Good," said Alia.

"What about Barry?" asked Bronwyn.

Alia sighed and told Bronwyn much of what she already knew; Barry had been diagnosed as having a nervous breakdown, but because of the things he was saying to the doctors, they wanted to more tests. Psychiatric tests.

"I don't want him to go to Banbridge. They'll put him away, and he'll be finished. He's not mad. He shouldn't have to go there!" Bronwyn's lip trembled at the thought of her twin locked away, and Alia nodded in agreement.

"I know, but he's in no state to make that decision. If we refuse, they might section him anyway."

"I want to see him. What time are they taking him there?" asked Bronwyn.

"First thing. I'm going down to Banbridge on the train. I think it would be good for Barry if you came, too."

Bronwyn agreed and they were both shocked when they looked at the clock to see it was nearing four o'clock.

"No point in getting any sleep now. How about I cook us a good breakfast and we get the first train out?" suggested Alia.

Bronwyn found that she was suddenly starving and, for the time being, she vowed to put all thoughts of Danny and Connor out of her mind. Today she was here for Barry.

* * * *

Neither Connor nor Rosina got any sleep that night. After Bronwyn's call, Connor had sat up thinking about the night's events. He knew the workings of the I.R.A better than most, and he knew he was in danger of being tracked down. At about quarter to five, Mary came downstairs.

"What's going on?" she asked, sitting down in the chair opposite him.

"Oh, Mam," Connor sighed, shaking his head. "I think I'm in trouble."

Mary's face dropped and she reached over to take his hand. "Tell me," she demanded.

Connor took a deep breath and told her everything that had happened that night. When he came to the part where the man in black had shot at him, Mary pulled her hand away from his and buried her face in her hands. He realised that she was crying and he moved over to hug her.

"I'm sorry, Mam. I never meant for this to happen, but I'm scared and I don't know what to do." He slumped back on the couch. "I might have to take Rosina and move away."

Mary looked up then and, through her tears, she smiled sadly at him.

"If I tell you a story, Connor, a true one, about your dad and me, it might make your decision to move away a little easier."

Connor leaned forward with interest. Although he knew his father had been Catholic, he didn't know the story of how he had died; it was something Mary had always refused to discuss with him over the years.

Mary repeated to Connor the story that she had told Rosina only a week before. When she was done, she turned to her son and saw that he was sobbing quietly, shedding tears for the father that he had been denied the chance to know.

"I don't want that to happen to you, son," she said and her voice broke. "Even if it means you're not here with me, I'd rather you move away than be buried next to your da."

They sat in silence for a long while, each lost in their own private thoughts about Billy Dean until the dawn light filtered through the curtains. Eventually Connor looked up at his mother and cracked a weak smile.

"New York, huh?" he said.

"Billy had been there. He had Irish relatives there, and it seemed like the best place to go," replied Mary.

"I like the idea," said Connor. "I'm going to speak to Rosina. It might be good for her to get away, too."

Chapter Thirteen

Connor's Escape

Rosina had spent the night in bed, but not sleeping. A thousand thoughts whirled around her mind; poor Danny, although he could have killed Connor it was still *Danny*, her friend from childhood, and whatever he had become, it didn't change the fact that he was now dead.

But still in the front of her mind was the terrible truth about her own heritage. It wasn't fair; she didn't need or even particularly want a father. Bronwyn and Connor had managed quite nicely without theirs, but to find out that her own had been a monster, who had attacked her mother was something she was finding incredibly hard to fathom. And with each morning that she woke, the depression was pulling her further down to a place where she couldn't find the strength or inclination to climb back out of to resume a somewhat normal life. She had a ton of questions that she wanted to know. Did she look like him? Did she have any of his traits or features? What was his name and, now that he was a grown man, was he paying penance for what he had done in his youth? But another visit to Kathleen was out of the question. Her mother, someone who had been a distant figure all of her life, was now, in Rosina's eyes, just a victim—just a sad, old lady who had been eaten up by the bitterness of Rosina's being.

Rosina sighed and pulled the quilt over her head as the sun rose. She couldn't face another day, another day of trying to keep the tears at bay, trying to be normal.

It was just too tiring.

The way out, when it came to her, was so simple that she wondered why she hadn't thought of it before. Throwing the duvet aside, she sat on the side of the bed and pondered upon the solution that she had devised. Could she do it?

"Yes. Yes, I can," she whispered to herself and decided that there was no time to waste.

Connor was making a mug of tea to take up to Rosina when she came hurtling down the stairs.

"Rosie!" he said as he heard her. "How are you feeling?"

She stopped in the doorway and observed him for a moment.

This was how it would be for the rest of their lives. Every day he would look at her with his eyes full of sympathy and wonder to himself if she was coping. No longer would they be equals, she would become the victim, and although he meant well, it was something she knew that she would not be able to live with.

So she smiled at him brightly.

"I'm fine," she said.

A look of surprise registered on his face and he walked over to her.

"Baby, you can't go out today. I need to speak to you about last night." He took her hands and looked her in the eye. "We might be in danger."

The thought had occurred to her as well and she nodded, but inside she was screaming. She had to go out, if she didn't put her plan into motion today she would start to think more rationally about it and lose her nerve.

"I know, I thought about it too. Let me just get the milk off the step and you can make me my tea, okay?"

Connor glanced down at the tea he had made. In his foggy state of mind, he hadn't even thought about milk. He gave a nervous laugh and turned back to the sink.

When Rosina opened the door she looked out into the street and closed the door quietly behind her. Then, as fast as she could, she ran down the street towards the town centre.

* * * *

The train journey to Banbridge was fraught with tension for Alia and Bronwyn. As they traveled north towards Belfast, Bronwyn stared out the window and watched the towns as they rolled past. She was finding it hard to believe where they were going; to see Barry, in a mental institute. It somehow didn't seem real. A thought struck her and she turned to Alia.

"Ma, what if it's hereditary?"

Alia, on the verge of dropping off, snapped her head up and looked at Bronwyn.

"What?"

"This thing, whatever's wrong with Barry, what if I could get it too?" Bronwyn was worried now and it showed on her face.

"It's not, you're fine, honest," replied Alia.

Bronwyn turned back to the window. Alia couldn't know that, but what else would she say?

Eventually they arrived at the town of Banbridge, and as they stood on the platform, they looked around for a taxi. Alia flagged one down and as they clambered in and told the driver their destination, Bronwyn saw the pitying look the cabbie gave them in his mirror. The drive was silent, and when they arrived, Bronwyn got out of the car and looked up at the huge building that was Banbridge House. It was a sobering sight, huge, grey, and set in what seemed like acres of land. It looked as depressing as Bronwyn had imagined. Few people were outside on the bitter December morning and, bracing themselves against the cold, Alia and Bronwyn hurried up to the front entrance. The first thing that Bronwyn noticed was the safety measures; glass screens around the reception desk, double locked doors that had security number pads above each door handle, and the guards that walked the corridors, burly looking men that could easily pass for night club bouncers. It was no surprise that few people ever left this place; there was certainly no chance of escape.

When the doctor treating Barry came to see them, he advised them that the rules of the house for new residents were only one visitor at a time.

"You go in first, Ma," said Bronwyn.

Alia gave Bronwyn's arm a grateful squeeze and followed the doctor down the hall.

Bronwyn wandered outside and sat on a bench near the reception area. She hadn't wanted to be the first to see Barry; if the truth were told, she was fearful of what she might find. Was he in a padded cell? A straightjacket maybe? Or doped up to the eyeballs, sitting at a table and dribbling, incoherent and unable to recognise her. For someone who had been her other half her whole life, it was a frightening thought. For if she lost Barry, her twin, it would be like losing a piece of herself.

Bronwyn turned her thoughts away from Barry and wondered what was happening with Danny's body. She wondered whether to tell Barry that his best friend was dead and decided against it; it would probably be a major setback, perhaps tip him over the edge, and she didn't want to be responsible for that. Memories of the night before came rushing back and she put her head in her hands. Like jet lag, it had suddenly crept up on her how serious the events had been; how she, Rosina, and Connor could have easily died out there.

Connor.

Like an angel's breath, his name whispered in her mind and she tried to push thoughts of him away. What was it about him anyway, that had her so hooked? He was everything in a man that she never went for; safe, reliable, loving, thoughtful…the list was endless. Before she could sink further into her reverie, Alia came out of the doors and Bronwyn stood up to meet her.

"He's asking for you," Alia said, and noting Bronwyn's alarmed expression she took her daughters hand. "It's okay, he's doing all right."

The doctor, waiting in reception, beckoned her over and as they walked down the hallway Bronwyn felt her heart thudding harder with each step she took. The doctor stopped at a door and showed Bronwyn through.

It was not a padded cell, there was no straightjacket, and Barry, sitting at a table, looked more relaxed than she had seen him in weeks. He stood up when he saw her and all of her concerns and fears washed away. She ran to him and hugged him tight.

"I was so worried about you!" she said, studying the bandages that were bound around his wrists. "Are you going to be okay?"

He pulled her over to the couch and sat her down. His eyes were eager and bright and she took his hands between hers.

"I'm fine, but Bronwyn, I need to tell you something. It's very important, and it's part of the reason I'm here," his voice was loaded with urgency and she nodded to show that she was listening.

"I've had a nervous breakdown. I was on the verge of something far bigger than that but, now that I'm here, I'm going to be okay. There were reasons for me being like this, and I'm going to explain them to you because I don't want you to be in any danger. You're smart, Bron, and I need you to help me to work out what to do next."

Eyes wide, Bronwyn glanced back towards the door to make sure the doctor had left them alone. The room was empty, except for the two of them.

"Go on," she said.

"You know I was a member of the I.R.A, well, I was actually there undercover. I've been an agent for the British government for nearly a year now. My job was to collect any information about the I.R.A's plans and take it back to my people, who would then use this information to stop attacks and the like. But it was getting harder, and I'm pretty sure that when I decided to quit both organisations I had been found out. That's why I'm here, it got too much and it nearly tipped me over the edge."

Bronwyn's eyes were wide and she stared at Barry in shock.

"But, I'd have known!" she spluttered.

"No, you didn't. Nobody could know, not you, or Ma, or anyone. The thing is, Bronwyn, now that the I.R.A know about me, it could put anyone around me in danger, and that includes Danny."

At the mention of his name, Bronwyn looked sharply up. "What?"

"They might think he was in on it. They know that he's a close friend and about his connection to you. If they suspect any involvement, they'll go after him now and ask questions later."

"Was Danny an agent, too?" Bronwyn asked, pale faced.

Barry shook his head impatiently.

"No, he was for real but they don't know that. They'll be suspicious of anyone linked to me." Barry noticed that Bronwyn was crying and he looked alarmed. "Hey? What's wrong?"

"Oh, Barry, I wasn't going to tell you…" she tried to choke back her tears but failed.

"What?" Barry paled considerably. "What is it?"

"Danny's dead," she whispered.

Barry turned away and stared out of the window.

"So, they got to him already," he said quietly.

"Christ, no, it was nothing to do with that," Bronwyn said. "I guess I should tell you the whole story, but it's between you and me okay? If it gets out that I was there when it happened, then I'm dead too."

She told Barry the tale of the night before, her connection with Stu and her instinct to run into the camp when the first bombs had exploded. When he learned that Stu had shot Danny to save Bronwyn, the first tears fell.

"Jesus, how did it come to this?" he said softly.

Bronwyn had stood up and was pacing the room. Her priority now lay with Barry and her need to protect him. She knew what would happen to him if he returned to Crossmaglen; he would just be another sad story that might one day be talked about, like Connor's shooting or Danny's untimely demise. The death list went on forever and, in Northern Ireland, more names got added to it every day.

"How long are they keeping you here?" she asked suddenly.

Barry shrugged.

"They want to do a few more tests because of the palpitations I've been having, make sure I get some rest, and see if they can't stabilise my sleeping as well. Why?"

Bronwyn came over and sat back down next to him.

"I'm gonna put the word around that you're here. If you're in Banbridge, nobody will touch you, and we'll keep it that way until we can figure out what to do next." She looked at him and said fiercely, "You won't be another statistic, I won't have it."

Barry nodded, and for a while they sat together, neither saying anything until Barry spoke up.

"Ma told me about her friend," said Barry. "Cally? Yes, that was her name. I promise you this family won't end up torn apart like that. Don't you worry about me, Bronwyn. My head is in better shape than everyone thinks."

"I should go." Bronwyn stood up and before she left she hugged Barry tightly. "I'm glad you're on the mend."

Barry buried his head in Bronwyn's shoulder and blinked back tears.

"Love you, sis," he murmured as they finally separated.

As she left, Barry walked over to the window and watched her as she exited the building and ran over to their mother. Barry felt a huge sadness descend upon him as he watched them go. He wished he had been able to say goodbye properly because, as far as Barry was concerned, it was probably the last time he would see his mother and sister for a very long time indeed.

When Rosina came home the house was in darkness and she wondered where Mary and Connor were. The note on the kitchen table told her; Connor had taken Mary to her friend Meg's house where he had insisted she stay for the time being. According to the note, he would be back about seven, after making sure she had settled in. She glanced at the clock and saw it was just after five; no time to waste then.

She shrugged off her coat and ran upstairs to the bedroom, where she emptied the contents of her carrier bag onto the bed and sorted through them. She stood the bottle of water she had bought on the bedside table and hurriedly changed into her pajamas. That done, she crawled into bed, poured a glass of water and took out the letter she had spent most of the day writing. It was already in an envelope with Connor's name on the front, and she propped it up against the lamp. Next, slowly and methodically, she took the five packets of paracetamol tablets she had bought and counted out fifty of them. Although she had a total of one hundred twenty-five tablets, Rosina reckoned fifty would be enough.

This little pile of paraphernalia—the tablets, the letter, and the bottled water—had been how Rosina had spent her last day.

She knew that chemists would only sell so many packets of painkillers in one go to a customer, so she had visited five pharmacies around Crossmaglen to purchase her desired amount. Then, walking aimlessly, she had planned her own death with meticulous precision. How many pills, that was the question? Not enough and she might just wake up in the morning with something that felt like a stinking hangover. Too many and she might vomit them back up before they could work. She finally decided on fifty, and if they weren't working she had another seventy-five as back up. The letter, ah, now that had not been so easy. How did one explain to their nearest and dearest that they had simply lost the desire to live? So, all afternoon she had sat in the Cross Café, where she had gone for breakfast with Mary and drank endless cups of coffee, as she composed her final letter. Eventually she had finished, and now she just had to take those pills, one by one until she drifted off to sleep and wouldn't have to wake up to the nightmare that had become her life.

Rosina frowned as she looked at the clock. It was now nearing five thirty, and the last thing she wanted was for Connor to arrive home early and rush her to the hospital; waking up with her stomach pumped would be too much to bear.

Taking a deep breath Rosina took the first pill and swallowed. Then another…three, four, five, six. The seventh pill made her gag and she threw back more water. Eight, nine, ten, eleven. On the eighteenth pill she had a moment of panic, asking herself, *Is this what I really want?* Then she closed her eyes and pictured Kathleen, envisioned her the last time she had seen her in the kitchen, calling her devil's spawn and admitting she had never loved her daughter. It was enough to spur her on. Nineteen, twenty, twenty-one…

After pill number forty-six, Rosina couldn't face swallowing any more. Her throat felt raw, so she slipped down beneath the covers and turned on her side to look at the clock. The digits were fuzzy, but she thought it said six-fifteen. She turned back over to stare up at the ceiling.

How will it be when I die? I don't want Connor to come in and see me with my eyes rolled back in my head, all glassy eyed and looking stoned.

With that thought, Rosina reached out and pulled the quilt over her head, so none of her could be seen. It was dark now, and she couldn't work out if it was because she was under the quilt or because her eyes were closed. Now her eyes were heavy, the pills were winning and everything was getting hazy. As she slipped under she let out a little cry, "Connor…"

Around ten minutes later, Jason Brady stormed up the street towards Connor Dean's home. He was alone, except for his Thompson sub-machine gun, and that was the way he preferred it. *If there was a job that needed doing, trust nobody but yourself.* Mickey had come through with the goods; he had confirmed that it had been Connor Dean who had witnessed the attack on the Crossmaglen army barracks and, once he had received verification, it was all Jason needed.

On his journey on foot from his house, he hadn't met anyone, and now he had arrived. He looked at the house and saw a lamp in the upstairs window. Before he went inside, he circled the perimeter of the house, peering in all of the windows. Well, if anyone else was in there with the Prod, then they would get it too. He marched up to the front door and leaned back on one leg, aiming his other to give the door a good kick. The door went flying inwards. Once in, he knew he had no time to waste and he sprinted upstairs, walked the length of the landing, kicking in all of the doors as he went. The final door he opened was the room at the front of the house, where he had seen the light on, and as he towered in the doorway he laughed aloud at what he presumed was Connor hiding under the bedclothes.

"Fucking pussy," he said and opened fire.

* * * *

On the main road that led into Protestant territory was a turning that the locals called The Rise. It was a hill and halfway up, anybody travelling, either by foot or by car, could look down onto the houses that nestled together. Connor did this now, on his return from taking his mother to Meg's house. After the mile or so he had walked, he paused on The Rise to look down at his house as he always did when taking this route home. As he stood and looked at his house, he was pleased to see the soft glow of the lamp in the bedroom that Rosina had claimed as her own. He was glad she was home; he had been worried when she had gone off this morning on her own. As he was just about to resume his walk he stopped and glanced back down to his house as a flash of light caught his eye. He squinted and looked carefully; there it was again!

Suddenly, he knew. The illumination in the bedroom window, it was just like he had seen in the barracks the night before.

It was machine gun fire.

"Fuck, no! Christ, no!" he shouted, and broke into a run.

It was another ten-minute walk from The Rise to his house, but Connor broke the speed record as he sprinted along, not noticing when he once again pulled the stitches and blood trickled down his leg.

The front door stood open and little wisps of smoke curled down from upstairs. Connor didn't even stop to think somebody could still be in his house. He hurtled upstairs and into Rosina's bedroom, and the sight that met him made him slump to the floor.

The bed—the big double bed that Rosina had loved—was filled with bloodstained bullet holes. Noting that the room was empty except for him, Connor crawled over to the bed and, whimpering, he pulled away the quilt.

Rosina lay underneath it, quite dead in her pink pajamas that were now stained an ugly red colour. He let go of the quilt and turned away, putting his hands to his head and pulling his hair. His face contorted with pain as he glanced back towards Rosina. He let out a yell of pure anguish. On his hands and knees, Connor edged back to Rosina and gathered her up in his arms. He buried his face in her hair and sobbed out her name, over and over.

As he held her, he noticed a heap of bottles that lay half-hidden under the bed and, still holding Rosina with one arm, he leaned down and knocked them out so he could see better.

Paracetamol bottles, five in all, which certainly hadn't been there that morning.

Carefully laying Rosina back down on the bed, he bent down to pick them up when the envelope on the bedside table caught his eye. It was addressed to him and he picked it up, trying not to dirty it with his bloodstained hands. Carefully, he opened it, and as he read it, he slumped back against the bed.

Dear Connor,

It's a coward's way out I know, but I can see nothing else in my future except the image of who I am and where I come from. Even you, who made me happier than I ever deserved or expected, cannot take away what I have become since I found out the truth.

I love you so much that I'm letting you go.

I only ask that you do the same for me.

Love...Forever,
Rosina

Connor let the letter drop from his hands and watched it as it landed amongst the empty pill bottles.

"She was already dying!" he whispered, and then, louder. "She was already dying!"

He began to chortle, not through humour or mirth, but with sadness and incredulity at the irony of it. And the harder he laughed, the more hysterical his laughter became.

It was a long time later, hours, in fact, when he stopped laughing and the full extent of what had happened hit him.

Rosina—his Rosie—was dead, and the perpetrators thought that they had killed him. This meant that he wasn't in any immediate danger, but, once they found out they had killed the wrong person, they would be back for him. Realising that he should get out of the house, he stood up. The carrier bag that Rosina had transported her goods in laid by the bed. He scooped up the Paracetamol bottles and Rosina's letter to him, and wondered where to go. Of all of his mates he couldn't think of one that would be able to help him, tell him what to do next. He didn't want to go to Meg's; it wouldn't do to put his mother in any more danger. It only took a moment more of mentally running through a list of his friends before Bronwyn's name came to mind. He took one last look around the room then leaned over and kissed Rosina tenderly. When he felt that he was about to lose control again, he bolted from the house and into the dark night.

* * * *

Alia had booked herself into a bed and breakfast so she could be near to Barry while he was in Banbridge House, and Bronwyn had not been home long when there was a frantic hammering at the door. Cautiously, she opened it a crack and was shoved backwards into the hall as Connor came crashing in. She took one look at him, sweating, bloodied, and disheveled and pulled him into the lounge, kicking the door shut after him.

"I'm real sorry, Bronwyn, I didn't know where else to go," he said.

"Bloody-hell, Connor, are you okay? Where's Rosie?" she asked.

At the mention of Rosina's name, a transformation came over Connor. He screwed his face up, clenched his fists, and Bronwyn stared on in horror, as tears ran down his cheeks. She knew straight away, but still she asked him.

"Connor? What's happened to her?" She pulled him down onto the sofa and sat beside him.

"Dead…" he managed, before a barrage of sobs escaped him.

Bronwyn slumped back in the chair while Connor broke down in front of her. She felt nothing, with all of the revelations of the past few weeks, Danny, and Barry, this latest news just left her numb.

"She can't be…" she trailed off, closing her eyes.

Rosina, her best friend for her entire life, *couldn't* be dead.

Suddenly she sat up.

"How?" she demanded.

Connor got his tears under control and handed her Rosina's note. She read it grimly and then handed it back.

"But there's more," Connor said, his voice hoarse with emotion. "When I was nearly home, I saw gun fire from the bedroom window. She was in bed, dying, and whoever did this thought it was me in that bed."

"Christ, Connor, I don't know…" Bronwyn stood up and stalking over to Alia's drinks cabinet, she poured herself a tumbler of vodka.

She couldn't think clearly and, as the drink burned her throat, she handed the rest of the glass to him.

"We need to think. They'll come back for you," she said, more to herself than to Connor. "You're not to go home. You should have left already." She glanced at him, almost accusingly.

He pulled an envelope out of his pocket and handed it to her.

"What's this?"

She opened it and when she saw the two plane tickets, she sat heavily back on the sofa.

"I just got them today. The flight's tomorrow. Now what am I going to do?" he asked with unconcealed dismay.

"You were going to New York?" she asked him as she read the destination on the tickets.

Connor nodded and told her of his late father's plans to leave Crossmaglen for New York with Mary, and how he had been killed before they could flee the country.

"You must go. My ma's friend is in New York, and I'm sure she would see you all right."

Bronwyn was thinking fast now, planning for Connor, as he was in no state to arrange anything himself.

"With any luck nobody will realise you're still alive and when they do, you'll be long gone. Does your ma know about this?"

He nodded.

"Right. Well, you can't go back to the house. We'll kit you out in some of Barry's things. Then, first thing tomorrow, you can leave and by tomorrow night you'll be in New York."

Connor leaned forward as he was struck with inspiration and he grabbed Bronwyn's hand.

"Come with me," he said urgently. "Leave this shit hole behind you and come to America with me."

Bronwyn was stunned at his proposal and pulled her hand away from his.

"I can't. I've got Barry to worry about. I can't leave Ma on her own," she exclaimed.

Connor sat back and ran his hands through his hair.

"I'm sorry," he said. "I wasn't thinking."

They sat in silence until Bronwyn went upstairs to pack some of Barry's clothes for Connor to take with him. As she packed, she thought about what Connor had said. What would he have done if she had accepted? But, as much as she hated the thought of sending him off on his own, she couldn't leave—no way.

With a small bag packed, she took it downstairs and left it in the hall. She went back into the lounge and stopped in the doorway when she realised Connor had fallen asleep on the couch. Rather than wake him, she fetched a blanket and, pulling it over him, sat down next to him. Poor Connor. From the look of the dried blood crusting around the top of his boot, it looked like his leg was bleeding again. She would have to patch him up before he left in the morning. Her eyes traveled up to his face and even now, despite the tragedy that had befallen them, just looking at him sent a tremor through her. His eyelids fluttered rapidly and she wondered if he were dreaming. As she got up, she noticed the two plane tickets on the floor. Heading upstairs, she left them both on top of his bag.

Back in her room, Bronwyn made a telephone call to Cally in New York. Once she had explained who she was and why she was calling, Cally, well versed in the troubles of her home country, assured her that she would look out for Connor and try to set him up with a place to stay, and maybe a job. Bronwyn thanked her and hung up the telephone. Her hand hovered over it as she debated whether to call the police. She decided against it. The longer Rosina's body went undiscovered, the better chance Connor had of getting away safely. It was a terrible thought, but she knew that Rosina would understand. As Bronwyn crawled into bed, she called her mother at the bed and breakfast in Banbridge. Alia was understandably devastated; she had known Rosina since childhood, and as she wept over the telephone line, Bronwyn felt strangely detached.

Once her mother had calmed down, Bronwyn told her what Connor's plans were and that she had phoned Cally in advance. Alia told her that she had done the right thing.

"He asked me to go with him," Bronwyn said and twisted the phone cord around her finger as she waited for her mother's reply.

"And?" Alia asked.

"I said I couldn't, what with Barry and all…"

"Baby, oh, God, Bronwyn, I wish you bloody would go," Alia's voice was thick with tears and at the other end of the telephone Bronwyn started in surprise.

"Go? But, I thought—"

"Oh, sweetheart, if I had the chance I'd get out of this Godforsaken place and make a new life. As much as I love my country, it's so full of heartache and pain. Look at Cally's family, Danny, Rosina, and Kathleen."

"Oh, Ma, I can't, not just yet," replied Bronwyn and she heard her mother heave a heavy sigh at the other end.

They hung up after that, with Bronwyn promising to call the next day to find out more news of Barry.

Bronwyn awoke the next morning and, for a second, everything seemed normal. Then she remembered. Rosina was dead, and Connor was in her lounge, sleeping in his grief. The first thing that she noticed as she hurried down the stairs was the bag that she had packed was no longer there. With a feeling of trepidation, she opened the lounge door.

Connor was gone, the blanket folded up neatly next to the couch.

"Shit," she muttered, and for a long while she stood looking at the place where he had slept last night.

Eventually she went into the kitchen and flicked the switch on the kettle. It wasn't until she sat down with a mug of tea that she saw the envelope on the kitchen table. She put her tea down and ripped it open. A letter, hastily written, and a plane ticket to New York fell out. With shaking hands she picked up the letter and began to read.

Dear Bronwyn,

Thank you for being there last night, and please thank Barry for his clothes.

I left early this morning so I could get to the airport without anyone seeing me.

I won't come back here, I can't come back as you know, so I'll try to pick up the pieces and start a new life away from Crossmaglen.

Bronwyn, you must realise by now that you can't change peoples' perceptions of who we are, and I ask that you, too, leave Crossmaglen before it crushes your spirit, because that would really be a terrible thing. I've left you the ticket, and if you change your mind about coming with me, then the plane leaves at midday.

Please, for your own sake, get out of here.
Connor

Bronwyn laid the letter out on the table and picked up the ticket. It was a life-changing moment. She knew that, and as she glanced at the ticket, she frowned and let out a sigh.

In her last year at high school she had completed an English project on a British mountaineer called Alison Hargreaves, who had actually died on the mountain K2. Alison had a motto, which for some reason had stuck in Bronwyn's head and had been a pearl of wisdom she had carried with her since.

Take the hardest path. If you fail, at least you know you tried. If you don't, you'll always wonder.

Bronwyn had lived by the rule of applying that statement to everything she did, but it had never been truer than it was now. Since her childhood she had been on the same road, and now she had come to a fork in the path. Staying in Crossmaglen was the easy option, and with sudden clarity, she knew what she had to do.

The taxi ride to Belfast Airport seemed to take hours, and Bronwyn leaned over the seat, glancing nervously at the meter. It was already standing at forty-three pounds and, although she now had seven hundred with her in cash, she didn't want to spend it all on a cab fare. At ten past eleven the cab pulled up outside the airport. Bronwyn threw the money at the driver and raced up to the flight desk, slapping the ticket down in front of the startled man behind the desk.

"Am I in time? I'm not too late, am I?" she babbled to the attendant.

He looked at his watch and then took her ticket.

"You might be in time but you really need to get to that boarding gate," he said, handing her the boarding pass.

She grabbed it and raced through the airport, praying that the plane wouldn't leave without her.

Connor let all of the other passengers onto the plane first and, when the final call came for his flight, he picked his bag up and looked around at the now empty departure lounge. He thought she might have changed her mind, but it looked like he was heading to New York on his own.

As he turned to board the plane, he suddenly heard the sound of someone running down the corridor that led to the departure lounge and he stopped to listen. When Bronwyn rounded the corner, sprinting like an Olympic champion, he dropped his bag to the floor and felt immense relief as she ran towards him.

Feet pounding the floor, Bronwyn fully expected to see an empty departure lounge when she came running in. But he was there, waiting for her, and as he came forward to meet her she threw her arms around him.

"You came!" She heard him cry and she held him tighter as they spun around, tangled in each other's arms.

He pulled away and picked up both the bags in one hand, taking her hand in the other.

"Come on," he said and together they ran through the door, towards the aeroplane that would take them to their new life.

Chapter Fourteen

New York

The funeral of Rosina James took place four days after her death on New Year's Day. The verdict was, of course, murder. With her body riddled with bullets, the coroner did not do a post mortem. He, like everybody else, presumed she had died at the hands of a revenge attack for the lifestyle she had chosen. There were few people at the burial. Kathleen was there, looking shell-shocked throughout the whole service, and Alia, on her own without Barry or Bronwyn. Mary had stayed away, and the people who knew that Rosina had been living with her assumed it was because of the disappearance of her son, which had occurred when Rosina had been murdered. Mary, of course, knew the truth of her son's whereabouts but she was telling that to nobody.

When the mourners drifted away, Alia went back into the church to utter up a prayer for Rosina, and also for Connor and Bronwyn. When she came back out of the church, she saw the stooped figure of a lady standing over Rosina's freshly dug grave. She knew instinctively it was Mary, Connor's mother, and she walked over to stand beside her.

"Missus Dean?" she asked, and Mary looked up, startled.

"I'm Bronwyn's mother," Alia said by way of explanation, and Mary relaxed and shook her outstretched hand.

"Shall we walk?" Alia asked, and together they made their way through the graveyard.

"Have you heard anything?" Mary asked.

"Yes, Bronwyn called me two days ago. They're staying with my friend, Cally, in New York, until they find their feet. I was hoping you were going to be here today. I brought Cally's number so you can call your son." Alia handed over a piece of paper and Mary took it silently.

They walked along through the stillness of the graveyard until Mary spoke up.

"You've got a real good girl there, and I'm glad she's with my boy."

"Me too. I told her to get out of here. I miss her like crazy, but she's made the right choice," replied Alia.

"You must be glad you've still got your boy with you," said Mary in reply.

Alia stopped walking and turned to face Mary.

"Barry's not at home. He's in Banbridge, and I don't know when he'll be back."

"I'm sorry," Mary was aware of Banbridge and why someone would be there.

"I'm sure he'll be well again soon." Alia held out her hand and Mary shook it solemnly. "And when you call Connor, make sure it's not from your house. They might have tampered with your phone lines."

Mary nodded and watched Alia walk away.

On the day of Rosina's funeral, Bronwyn sat alone in Cally's apartment and tried not think about her friend. Alia had informed her the burial was today, but, although she had not shed any tears for Rosina, she was still not ready to reflect on the fact that she was dead.

Things had happened so quickly since they landed in New York three days ago and made their way to Cally's home in downtown Manhattan. When they had left the airport and stood on the sidewalk, Bronwyn had been overwhelmed by the hustle and bustle of the city. After the sleepiness of Crossmaglen, it was a big change. They had hailed a taxi and arrived at Cally's, who had been surprised to see Bronwyn arrive with Connor, but had welcomed them both into her home.

Cally had done well for herself since leaving Belfast. She had married a rather well off businessman, Sam Mason, and they had set up home in Manhattan in a four-storey house. Sam worked for I.B.M and his highly paid job meant that Cally could enjoy the luxury of being a stay at home wife, something that she was quite content to do. Cally was also six months pregnant with their first child, and when Bronwyn learned this, she promised that they would be out of her hair as soon as possible. Cally was happy to have them around; she assured them it was nice to see someone from the place that, even after twenty years, she still thought of as home. When Cally led them upstairs, Connor and Bronwyn were stunned by the size of the fourth floor that was to be their temporary home. It had two bedrooms, which Bronwyn was quietly relieved about, and an ensuite bathroom for each bedroom. It even had its own lounge area, with windows that stretched from floor to ceiling, boasting panoramic views over the city.

Today was the first day that Bronwyn had been left alone. Cally was visiting Sam's relatives in Queens, and Connor was out looking for work. Connor and Bronwyn had not discussed their plans any further than finding work, and Bronwyn was worried about how to broach the subject. Was Connor intending to find a home for both of them to share? Or, now that they were here, did he expect them to go their separate ways?

Bronwyn sat on the wide window ledge and looked out across the city. She was confused and tired. She missed Barry and her mother, but most of all she missed Rosina. A vision of

Rosina flitted across her mind, a vision of her friend, slumped over her bed, riddled with bullets and blood. How had she felt when she had died? When the pills took effect and she closed her eyes for the very last time, was she regretting it? Did she think of Bronwyn, or Kathleen, or Connor? Did she wish for one last chance to try and resume her life as best she could?

I won't think about her…not yet.

She clenched her fists and leaned her head against the cold window, trying to think of something else, something to take her mind off the thoughts that ran through her head. She glanced at the clock and realised the funeral would be over by now. Had Kathleen attended? Most probably, doing her mourning-widow act, and pretending that she was devastated over the loss of the daughter who she had never loved.

Realising that she was close to breaking down, Bronwyn climbed off the ledge and reached for her coat. It was time to go and look for a job.

When Connor arrived back at the Masons' house, Cally told him that Bronwyn was out job hunting.

"Take some dinner with us, won't you?" she asked as she busied herself in the kitchen.

"I'm not all that hungry," he replied. "But, thanks anyway."

"Rubbish, you've not eaten a proper meal since you got here. You need to keep your strength up, lad."

Connor sat down at the kitchen table.

"What for?" he asked despondently.

Cally stopped her work and sat down opposite him, a sympathetic look on her face.

"To get through *this*," she said. "You're hurting right now and—believe me—I know just what you're going through."

"Oh yeah?" A glint of anger shone in his eye and he looked up at her. "How could you possibly know?"

"Because I lost my entire family at the hands of those bastards in Ireland, that's how," she replied and Connor, his anger forgotten, stared at her.

"What?"

"Bronwyn didn't tell you? I don't suppose I blame her. It's not something I like to tell people about, or else they start looking at you different."

"I didn't know... I'm sorry," he said, embarrassed to have snapped at her. "When was this?"

"Twenty years ago. I was the same age as Bronwyn and, if her mother hadn't been with me that night, I'd have been dead as well." Cally settled herself down and prepared to tell him the whole story. "It was a fire. Someone set fire to my house as my mam, dad, and three brothers were sleeping. When I came home the house was ablaze, smoke all over the street."

"And they couldn't save anyone?" Connor whispered.

"My mam was alive when Alia and I got here, and it was a terrible sight. On fire she was, at the bedroom window and she held Shane, my baby brother, out of the window and Alia went to catch him. I couldn't watch. My God, I closed my eyes and just prayed, but before Alia could catch Shane, the window blew from the heat and it knocked her right off her feet. So they all went, all dead and I left, like yourself, to start a new life." Cally took Connor's hand and smiled at him. "Now see, I'm a wife, nearly a mother, and I have a whole new family to take care of. I guess I'm trying to tell you that it does get better, you won't forget, but it'll get easier, and you'll move on."

"I guess, but Rosina...she was special." Connor smiled as he remembered. "She was so sweet. She wouldn't have hurt anything or anyone. I never knew anyone as kind or as good as her."

"She sounds very special. And I can't say anything to make it better for you, all you need is time."

"It was her funeral today," said Connor.

"I know, Alia told me over the telephone. And I know you're sad that you couldn't be there, but why don't you have a drink and remember her in your own way?"

Cally stood up and resumed her cooking. Connor nodded and made his way up to the fourth floor.

When Bronwyn came home it was late, almost ten o'clock, and seeing that the lights were out downstairs, she made her way directly up to the fourth floor, hoping that Connor was still up so she could tell him about her day. He was awake, but he didn't hear her come in. She put her bag on the table and watched him from the doorway as he sat, slumped over the table in the lounge area, a half empty bottle of whiskey in front of him. He had his back to her, and at first she thought he had fallen asleep, but then he reached for the bottle and poured another finger of whiskey into his glass. As she came into the room he heard her and turned around. He was drunk, she could see that now, and she stared at him uncertainly, trying to read his expression in the soft glow of the lamplight.

"Are you okay?" she asked eventually.

"Yes," he said shortly and turned back to stare down into his glass.

"You won't find any answers in there," she said, light-heartedly.

"There are no answers. Here, or anywhere else," he said, the pain that he was feeling apparent in his voice.

This was a Connor that she had not yet encountered. She had seen him sad, smiling, and serious, but not like this. His mood, she could tell, was black and his stance was that of a man in the throes of depression. She didn't like it, not one bit.

"Hey." She walked over to him and crouched down by his chair. "Talk to me, I don't wanna see you like this."

He turned to face her and for the first time she saw the fire in his eyes, and he appeared, just for a moment, like Danny used to look, when he was drunk and angling for a fight. Full of pent up aggression and anger.

"How do you want to see me, Bronwyn?" he asked, and just her name on his lips sent shivers down her spine.

"Hopeful, positive," she said. "You were so optimistic this morning."

He banged his glass down hard on the table and she jumped as the noise resounded off the walls.

"What the fuck have I got to be hopeful about? You tell me that," he shouted.

"Don't fucking take it out on me!" she shouted back. "Do you think I'm not angry? Or hurt, or upset, or lonely?"

"Why don't you show it then?" He was yelling now, not caring if he woke up the rest of the house with his rant. "You're so fucking cool all the time! Do you not realise what's happened to our lives? She was your best friend, all of your life she was there, and you've not even shed a tear!"

He stood up, knocking the chair over and she pulled herself up to face him.

"I can't think about it! I can't give myself that luxury yet, or I'll bloody crack!" She was angry now, and the blaze in her eyes matched his.

They faced each other, circling like warring lions, and without warning Connor suddenly lurched towards her, grabbing her face between his hands. There was a split second of hesitation before his mouth was on hers, and she was returning his kiss with more hunger and passion than she had ever felt before. His fingers knotted through her hair and as his lips traveled down her neck she closed her eyes in something close to ecstasy. Still fused together, they stumbled against the wall and she slid her hands up and under his shirt. His skin was taut and smooth. She moaned, with an almost animal sound, as his lips once again found hers. Suddenly a vision flashed through her mind and she pulled away from him.

"Rosina!" she cried. "We can't!"

At the sound of her name, Connor stopped and shook Bronwyn hard by her shoulders.

"Rosina's dead," he hissed, his face contorted with rage.

When he uttered the words it was as if Bronwyn had heard them for the first time and she stared at him, wide-eyed and unbelieving. Then, as it finally hit home, she crumpled as her legs gave way beneath her. Connor caught her and lowered her gently to the floor, where he fell to his knees beside her. She looked up at him, and the tears that she never thought would come spilled over. Connor, his anger depleted and now just feeling very sad, wiped the tears from her cheeks.

"Oh, God…" Bronwyn let out a high pitched shriek and covered her face with her hands.

Connor wrapped his arms around her and she fell against him, sobbing as if her heart would break. He whispered to her, inane, comforting words that meant nothing but soothed her nonetheless. They stayed like that, bound together in grief, until they heard the city come alive outside with the sounds of the early dawn.

* * * *

Back in Crossmaglen, Alia was getting anxious as she waited on the telephone for the daily report about Barry. Normally the doctor was with her within minutes to give her a full update on his tests and medicines. She had now been on hold for five minutes and was just about to hang up when Doctor Lough came on the line.

"Missus Ranger?" he asked and she confirmed that yes, it was she.

"Is Barry not with you?" he asked, and at these words her blood ran cold.

"Why would he be with me?" Her voice was abnormally high pitched and she cleared her throat.

"Missus Ranger, Barry discharged himself last night. It was against our advice but, as he was not sectioned, there was nothing we could do to keep him here."

"What time last night?" she asked.

"Around six. I'm sorry, but I presumed he would be coming straight home," the doctor said.

"Thank you, I'm sure he's on his way." Alia hung up the phone and chewed anxiously on her fingernail.

It was now ten in the morning; there were plenty of trains from Banbridge, and Barry should have been home by midnight, if he left at six. She sat down at the kitchen table and worried over what to do. She couldn't look for him, as he could have gone anywhere on a train, bus, or coach. Did he even have any money? Alia closed her eyes and rubbed her forehead. She couldn't stand if anything happened to Barry, not with Bronwyn gone as well. After another fifteen minutes of biting her nails and coming up with no solution, she was deliberating whether to call the police or not when the phone rang. Relief flooded through her and she snatched it up.

"Barry?" she asked.

"Missus Ranger, it's Doctor Lough again," the doctor's dulcet tones came over the line and she sighed with disappointment.

"Hello, Doctor. How can I help?"

"Well, one of the nurses was clearing out Barry's room and she's brought me a letter that is addressed to you. Just to let you know, I'll be forwarding it on to you, straight away."

"What does it say?" she cried, thinking of Rosina and her suicide note.

"I've not read it, Missus Ranger. It's addressed to you," Doctor Lough sounded affronted.

"Open it!" she pleaded. "Read it to me, it could be very important."

There was a sigh at the other end of the line and he cleared his throat as he prepared to read.

"'Ma, as you know by now, I've discharged myself. I can't come home, and I can't explain why in this letter, in case it gets into the wrong hands. Please, speak to Bronwyn and tell her to tell you everything.'"

"Is that all?" Alia was confused. What would Bronwyn know?

"The word 'everything' is underlined three times," the doctor said dryly.

"Thank you, it was good of you to call. Goodbye."

As soon as the dial tone sounded, Alia rang the number of Cally's home in New York.

"Hello?" It was Cally's voice, and Alia almost shouted down the line.

"Cally, I need to speak with Bronwyn, is she there?"

"Alia, of course, hold on."

Alia heard the sound of the phone being put down and then Cally calling for Bronwyn. Seconds later, Bronwyn was on the line.

"Ma?"

"Bronwyn, I've got a letter here from Barry. It says he's discharged himself from Banbridge, and that he's not coming home. It says you're to tell me everything."

193

There was a pause at the other end and then Bronwyn spoke up.

"Okay, I'll tell you. Are you sitting down?"

"Yes," Alia lied.

"Barry was in the I.R.A, undercover as an agent for the British government."

At Bronwyn's words Alia sank to the floor and gripped the phone, for fear that she would drop it in her shock.

"Ma?"

"Go on," Alia whispered faintly.

"He thinks he was found out. That was part of what pushed him over the edge, and if he came home, he knew he would be killed."

"And you knew this?" Alia asked in a shocked voice.

"Not until that day we went to visit him. I was as shocked as you, Ma. Where do you reckon he's gone?" Bronwyn asked.

There was silence as Alia thought about it, and then a smile came over her face as she figured the only place Barry would now go to.

"Don't get your hopes up, but I think I know where he might be headed," she said.

Bronwyn got it as well, and the excitement could be heard in her voice.

"New York?" she asked breathlessly. "You told him I was here, right?"

"That I did, baby. Don't get too excited. Remember he doesn't know where you're living, but please, please, keep your eyes open for him."

"Oh, I will but, Ma, I can't bear to think of you there, on your own," Bronwyn said mournfully.

Before she could reply there was a knock on the door. Alia leaned out into the hall and through the glass she saw Mary, Connor's mother.

"I'm not here alone," she said. "Mary's at the door. Hold on…" She put the phone down and opened the front door, gesturing for Mary to come in. "Bronwyn? I'm back. Like I said, I'm not alone so don't you worry about me. I'll call again, okay?"

"All right, Ma. Love you."

As she replaced the telephone, Alia turned to face Mary. Before she could invite the woman in for a drink, she felt a lump in her throat and realised that her hands were shaking.

"Are you okay?" Mary stepped forward, face concerned.

Alia shook her head and tried to get herself under control. This was a woman she barely knew. It wouldn't do to break down in front of her. Breathing deeply, she finally looked up and smiled. Mary seemed relieved that she wouldn't have to do the whole comforting thing. It was a trait of the Irish woman; strong, tough, and hard as nails. It was the way both had been raised and now, as Mary followed Alia into the kitchen, they dealt with a shock in the usual way.

"Let me put the kettle on for a nice cup of tea, and I'll tell you all about it."

* * * *

"So, did you find a job?"

Bronwyn had been trying to avoid Connor all morning. She had just returned upstairs to the fourth floor after Alia's telephone call and Connor cornered her in the lounge.

"Yesterday? No, but I gotta go back to this bar today. Someone said the manager is looking for staff." She edged past him and made her way to the window to look down into the street. "How did you get on?"

He followed her and stood behind her. Bronwyn glanced at his reflection in the glass and looked down.

"Nothing yet," he replied. "About last night…"

She turned round to face him. *Yes, what about last night?* One minute they had been locked in passion, the next she was a crying wreck on the floor. She was confused; he had been drunk and, in the cold light of day, he didn't seem so interested in her *that* way anymore.

"Let's forget about last night," she said. "I was upset, you were drunk…" her voice trailed off and she looked up at him, trying to work out what he was feeling.

Eventually, with a grim expression, he nodded and changed the subject.

"So, this bar, what time are you going? Do you think they'd speak with me as well?"

Her face brightened. To have Connor beside her in a new job would make it far less daunting.

"Come with me, we'll see what they say."

"What did your ma have to say?" he asked as he wandered over to the sofa.

"Barry's gone missing. He discharged himself," she said and leaned against the window. "He was afraid, you see. He thought that if he returned to Crossmaglen, he'd be killed."

Connor frowned.

"Why would he think that?"

Bronwyn came over to the couch and sat down next to him.

"He was working for the British government, undercover in the I.R.A, and he got found out," she said. "I'm just hoping he turns up here."

"Jesus, Bronwyn, I had no idea."

"Me neither," Bronwyn admitted. "Not until last week…" she trailed off. Had it only been a week since her life had been turned upside down?

"So, he might come here. What does he look like? I don't want to mistake him for someone looking to do me in," Connor made an attempt at humour and Bronwyn smiled in return.

"He looks like me." Bronwyn pulled her bag off the table and retrieved a photograph of her, Barry, and their mother.

Connor studied it and looked up.

"He does look like you." He handed the picture back. "I'd have known he was your brother without seeing that."

Bronwyn put the photo away, quietly pleased.

"Shall we go then? To the bar, I mean."

He nodded, and together they went to get their coats. As they walked out, Bronwyn hoped that some of the tension between them had cleared, and that they would eventually become proper friends.

* * * *

Back in the Crossmaglen barracks, life was slowly getting back to normal for Stu. After killing Danny, he had become filled with mixed emotions at what he had done. His fellow colleagues had done their best to make him see that if he hadn't shot Danny, Danny would surely have killed him. Of course, nobody else knew about Bronwyn, or the lad that had been with her in the barracks that night, and that was the way he intended to keep it. A week later and he was out of the base, on his way to see Bronwyn to make sure she was bearing up okay. He had no idea of where she lived, so instead he made his way to the Fox and Hound and asked for her there.

Lila, the landlady, looked Stu up and down and was immediately suspicious.

"What do you want with Bronwyn?" she asked.

The pub was empty except for the two of them, and he took a seat at the bar.

"I heard about her boyfriend, and I wanted to check she was okay," he said. "Will she be in later?"

"No," Lila said shortly.

"Well, can you maybe give me her telephone number? Or her address?" he asked, slightly exasperated.

Lila banged the tray of glasses on the bar and turned to face him.

"Look, Bronwyn's done a runner. Left me right in the lurch, too, so it's no good asking me where she is."

Stu frowned and gave a heavy sigh. There would be no chance of finding her now; she may have even left Crossmaglen altogether.

Lila saw his disappointed expression and her tough exterior melted somewhat.

"Look, her ma might know. Go visit her." Lila scribbled an address on a beer mat and passed it over. "And, if you find her, tell her to get her arse back to work."

Stu thanked her and hurried outside. He had an idea of the location of this address, having remembered it from one of the raids he had done during his first week here. It was not far on foot. Eventually he found the right house and knocked on the door. A lady opened it, and it was clear from her looks that she was Bronwyn's mother.

"I'm looking for Bronwyn," he said.

"Why?" she asked, possessing much of the suspicious attitude that Lila had given him minutes earlier.

"I'm a friend." He stepped forward and held out his hand. "I'm Stu."

At the sound of his name her expression changed, and recognition filtered over her face.

"Stu, well, you'd better come in." She held the door open and, surprised, he followed her in.

Stu knew that the locals had just cause to be apprehensive about any of the British soldiers that served in their country. The only time that soldiers usually came into these houses was when they were working with the R.U.C., and that was to make dawn raids, smashing up their homes while looking for arms or I.R.A weaponry. Ever mindful of this, Stu took care to appear as unthreatening as possible towards this lady. He stood awkwardly in the kitchen doorway until Alia beckoned him to a chair, and he took a seat opposite her.

"Bronwyn told me everything that happened the other night," said Alia. "I should thank you, for saving her."

Stu was quite surprised; the events of a week ago in the army camp were not something most girls would tell their mothers.

"There's no need for thanks. I was just doing my job," he said uneasily. "But, is she okay?"

"Bronwyn's fine. She's left Crossmaglen, and although I can't tell you where she is, I know that she's okay."

Stu nodded, he understood that.

"She's a fine girl. Wherever she is, I'm sure she'll be just fine. From what I know of her, Bronwyn's strong. She's…special, I guess."

Alia looked up sharply and uttered a strange laugh.

"Funny, that's what she said about you."

He left not long after, but not before giving his number to Alia and telling her that if she ever was in need of any help, she was to call him.

She took it without looking at it, and he wondered if she would throw it away just as soon as look at it.

As the door closed behind him, it also closed on the very short chapter of his life that had been Bronwyn Ranger.

Chapter Fifteen

Beginnings

The bar was packed, and Bronwyn yelled over the counter.

"I need some change!" She held her money belt up in the air and waved it.

Connor, serving customers at the other end of the bar, caught her eye and grinned. She smiled back, tapped her watch and he nodded. Reaching over to turn the music down, he shouted out to the occupants of the bar.

"Time's up, folks, drink up and clear outta here!"

Bronwyn giggled at the groan that resounded around the room and took the bag of coins from Lucia, the owner of Zak's, the bar that both she and Connor had worked in for five months now. As the bar slowly cleared of people, Bronwyn took a moment to sit back and think about how much her life had changed in just five months.

There was the job, to start with. Lucia had hired both Connor and Bronwyn on the spot, and they had never looked back since. She reminded Bronwyn a lot of Lila, the Irish landlady of the Fox and Hound back home, although the pub itself couldn't be further from her old local. It wasn't a pub, which was the first thing Lucia had drummed into them. It was a *bar*, and due to its perfect location amid the office blocks in Manhattan, its main attraction was for businessmen and women after a long day at the office.

Their home had changed too. They no longer resided at Cally's, and instead they had rented a two-bedroom apartment over on 42nd Street, moving in together three months ago. The night that Cally had given birth to her daughter, Bella, Bronwyn had said to Connor that they should seriously think about moving out. Cally and Sam had already spoken of their plans to turn the fourth storey of the house into a nursery, although she had said that they were in no hurry, as the baby would sleep in with them for at least a few months. It was the subject that Bronwyn had been dreading, and many a sleepless night had been spent wondering what their living arrangements would be when the time came that they no longer *had* to live together. Connor had solved that, however, when he proposed that they share an apartment. After all, he had said, what would be the point in paying two rents when they could divide everything equally. Bronwyn had been cynical at first, but it had worked out better than she ever expected. There had been no repeat performance of what had happened on the night of Rosina's funeral, and it had never been mentioned again between them. Still though, sometimes when Bronwyn looked at him, she felt that familiar pang of longing. But Connor was a friend now, her *best* friend, and she had vowed when they moved in together that she would do nothing to jeopardise that. The grief of Rosina's untimely death was relaxing its grip on them both, and in the last few weeks they had found that they were able to speak of her again without dissolving into tears. The healing process was well underway.

But, as if to replace the pain that Bronwyn had felt about Rosina, there was another disappointment. Barry had never turned up in New York, nor had he returned home to Crossmaglen. Neither Alia nor Bronwyn had heard any news of him now in over six months. Bronwyn woke each morning with the hope that today would be the day that Barry would arrive. She found herself, more and more lately, staring at every dark haired man on the street, in the bar, or in a restaurant, in the hope that it was he, but it never was. Connor was a big support in her heartache at losing Barry, and he constantly consoled her with the suggestion that he was hiding away, in a new life away from danger.

"Hey!" Connor's voice broke her out of her reverie and she looked up. "Get over here and help me, you slacker!"

She laughed aloud and got up from her chair.

The biggest difference in her new life was Connor. It was as though he had been repressed in Ireland and, here in the vivacious city that was New York, he had come alive. Never before would she imagine that he would be joking or laughing with the customers who, along with the regulars in the bar, had become very fond of the Irish pair. But although he had grown in confidence over the last six months, he still had the same traits that had appealed to Bronwyn. When they left the bar after work each evening and walked the ten blocks home, it was as if he left his new personality at Zak's, becoming attentive and caring again, but never to the extent that it could be misconstrued as something more.

"Ah, get home, you two, I'll finish up here," said Lucia, shooing them away with the towel that she was using to wipe the tables.

"Cheers, Luce," said Connor, handing Bronwyn her coat. "See you Monday."

It was Saturday night, and even though it was nearly midnight, the streets were still busy in the city that never sleeps. Bronwyn loved Saturdays, mainly because the next day was Sunday, and it was the one night they didn't have to work. When they left work on Saturday nights they always made a point of stopping at Cally's house to pay her a visit. Cally was a night owl, never going to sleep before the early hours of the morning. During those nights when Sam and Bella were sleeping, she was glad of the company and the gossip that they always bought her from the bar.

Now, as Cally opened the door, looking for the entire world like it was first thing in the morning and not the time for sleeping, she smiled widely at the couple she had grown so fond of, and let them in.

"I'm glad you've come. Connor, Sam has something he wants to talk to you about. Go upstairs, he's waiting for you."

"Does nobody in this place ever sleep?" Connor asked, and right on cue Bella started to wail. They all laughed.

Connor went upstairs to see Sam, and Bronwyn went through to the kitchen. Moments later, Cally came back in holding Bella and Bronwyn held her arms out to be passed the baby.

When they were all settled, Cally leaned back in her chair and sighed.

"This is the life, Bronwyn. This is all that matters."

"Bella?" asked Bronwyn, staring down at the baby who was falling asleep.

"Bella, Sam, friends…you and Connor have become a big part of our lives, you know," replied Cally.

"We couldn't have managed here without your help. You and Sam have been so good to us," said Bronwyn.

"I'm glad you came round tonight. We wanted to give you these." Cally reached behind her and passed two envelopes across the table, one addressed to Connor and one to Bronwyn.

"What are they?" Bronwyn asked.

"Invitations, to Bella's christening in July. We want you both to be there," Cally paused. "As godparents."

Bronwyn's mouth dropped open in shock before a smile lit up her face.

"Oh, Cally, do you really mean that?"

"Yes, I do. I can't think of anyone better suited than you two." A mischievous look came over Cally's face. "Speaking of which, what are you two playing at anyway?"

Bronwyn shifted the baby in her arms and looked confused.

"What do you mean?"

"You and Connor, anyone can see he's mad about you. Why are you not together?"

"Cally! It's not like that!" retorted Bronwyn. "He's my friend."

"Surely you've thought about it, I mean, he's a good-looking lad," Cally turned serious.

"Sure, I've thought about it. We came close once as well, the night of Rosina's funeral. But since then…we don't speak about it. It's not going to happen." Bronwyn smiled and shrugged.

Cally came around the table and took the sleeping Bella from Bronwyn's arms.

"Give it time. I'm not usually wrong about these things. Oh, here they are!"

Connor and Sam came into the room and, by the look on Connor's face, Bronwyn could see he was delighted to have been asked to become Bella's godfather. Connor also had more news for Bronwyn and he sat down at the seat that Cally had vacated.

"Sam's brother is opening a bar, in Times Square, and he's asked me to manage it."

"Connor!" Bronwyn clapped her hands together. "That's fantastic!"

Both Connor and Bronwyn shared the vision of someday jointly owning their own bar. With Connor now being given a management position, it meant that they were one stop closer to realising their dream.

As Sam sat with them at the table while Cally took Bella upstairs, Bronwyn watched Connor carefully as he chatted with Sam. Why had Cally said he was mad about her? That was something she had not seen for herself, and except for that one night of drunken near-madness on his part, she had presumed that her feelings, long buried, had always been one sided. Cally was just a hopeless romantic, she told herself. Connor cared for her, of that she was certain, but not in the way Cally imagined.

Later, as they made their way home, Bronwyn was unusually quiet. When Connor asked if she was all right, she nodded.

"I'm looking forward to the christening. I'm going to be a godmother! Probably the nearest I'll get to being a mother," she said.

"Bullshit!" Connor protested. "Someday you'll be like Cally, and you'll make the best mother in the world."

She smiled, happily basking in his praise, and she linked her arm through his, chatting the rest of the way home.

When they arrived at the apartment on 42nd Street, Bronwyn went straight to bed. Connor sat up for a while, as he usually did at night when he wasn't tired, and looked out into the street. It was getting warmer now; summer was upon them, and he opened the window to let the refreshing night air into the room. A while later he made a cup of coffee and took it to his room. He stopped at Bronwyn's bedroom door, which was open, and for a while he stood, sipping his coffee, watching her while she slept. She too, had apparently felt the warm night and had thrown off her cover in her sleep. She lay in her usual night attire, tracksuit and vest, and her arm was thrown up to rest on the pillow over her head. Bronwyn never closed her curtains, and the moonlight filtered through the window, illuminating one side of her with its silver light. She was beautiful, Connor thought. Asleep, awake, drunk, sober, sad or happy, whatever she was never took away an ounce of her beauty. She stirred in her sleep and he moved back into the shadows. When she didn't wake, he waited for a moment before moving on to his room, where he stood by the window while he finished the coffee. He often remembered the night that they had kissed. Although they had gotten over that and become as close as any two people could be without being lovers, he regretted that they had never taken that step. But it was too late now, too much time had passed, and it was obvious to him that she was happy with the way things were between them. Connor climbed into bed and lay looking up at the ceiling. He consoled himself, as he always did, that it was better to have her in his life as a friend than not to have her at all.

* * * *

In Crossmaglen, not much had changed. If anything, events had only worsened since Bronwyn and Connor left. As Bronwyn was finishing work, Alia had just gotten up and collected the newspaper from the front door mat. Now she sat at the kitchen table and stared at the newspaper that lay before her. The headline jumped out at her.

SANDS DEAD.

She glanced over to the back door where the pile of papers from the last two weeks had stacked up. The headline of only a week ago glared at her.

SANDS IN COMA, NEARS DEATH.

Now death had taken him, the young man who was twenty-seven years old. He had died for the love of his country, for his cause of an independent Ireland.

Ever since the hunger strike had begun in Long Kesh sixty-six days ago, the country had gone mad. Riots were a daily occurrence, people were utterly incensed that their hero had achieved martyrdom and had been allowed to stare death in the face by the British government. There would be worse trouble now, and it wouldn't end, because there were nine other men on a hunger strike and they would follow their leader to his death. For each man who died there would be untold riots. All Alia could do was thank God that her children were not here to be involved in it.

When the news of Bobby Sands' death reached Bronwyn in New York, she telephoned Alia immediately.

"Is it very bad there?" asked Bronwyn, fearfully.

Alia hesitated before answering, not wanting to worry her.

"It's not so bad here. Belfast is seeing the worst of it."

"It's so sad, Ma. He was just a little bit older than me." Bronwyn twisted the phone cord around her finger. "Such a waste of a life."

"He died for what he believed in, and that's admirable. But you're right, it's very sad."

After chatting some more about Bobby Sands and the goings-on at Long Kesh, they hung up, with promises to talk again soon.

Two days later, the funeral of Bobby Sands took place in Milltown Cemetery, Belfast. Alia, on her own in the house and jittery about the unrest outside, decided to attend. When she reached Belfast town centre, she was shocked to see the procession that lined the streets. Her throat burned with unshed tears at the untimely death of a young man, and with her children and everyone lost to her in her heart, she joined the crowd of one hundred thousand people, marching along to the sorrowful sound of the piper that led the procession.

That the funeral was besieged with members of the Irish Republican Army made no difference to Alia, and perhaps for the first time in her life she saw how passionately they felt about their desire for an independent Ireland.

As Alia saw the devastation Bobby's death caused, she wished more than ever for peace in her homeland, but knew that it would be a long time coming, if it ever came at all.

* * * *

Another two months passed, and not much had changed in their lives except Connor was now the manager of Mayfair, an elite restaurant and bar in Times Square. The bar was totally brand new, and Sam's brother, Carl, had given Connor a free hand in hiring staff and sorting out the opening night. Naturally, he had offered Bronwyn a job at Mayfair, but she enjoyed her work at Zak's so had decided to stay there. Now that Connor was working days, from around eight in the morning until well after noon, he noticed that he barely saw Bronwyn anymore. She still worked the night shift at Zak's, and was normally rushing around getting ready for work when he got home at night. Sunday, their favourite day, had not changed, and for that Connor was grateful. He would rise early, go down to the newsagent, and then to the supermarket a block away, to buy their breakfast. He would then return home and eventually the smell of the bacon and eggs would rouse Bronwyn from her slumber. She would stand sleepily in the kitchen, until he told her sit down and stop getting in his way. They would take a leisurely breakfast, then retire to the lounge, where they would take a couch each and devour the Sunday papers. A new tradition had been incorporated into their Sundays; Connor would stop at the video store on his way home from work Saturday night to pick up a film, which was always a surprise for Bronwyn, until Sunday afternoon when they watched it. Bronwyn was amused by his choice of films; sometimes they would be classics, like Casablanca, or An Affair to Remember. Other times, they would be action or horror movies. Bronwyn could sense his mood, based on what type of film he brought home. Around five, they would get ready to go out for dinner, their final Sunday treat, after which they would return home and relax on the porch steps until it was time for bed.

Now he clung onto their Sunday's spent together and valued them more than ever. Since Mayfair had opened, they were like ships that passed in the night, and that was why he was looking forward to this particular weekend. Today, Saturday, was his birthday, and tomorrow was Bella's christening. Tonight, he was planning to leave the restaurant early. This evening he and Bronwyn were going out for dinner with Sam and Cally. Bronwyn was already at home, getting ready for tonight, and he was just cashing up the afternoons takings at Mayfair, when Joe, one of the barmen, came into the office.

"Some guy looking for you, boss," said Joe.

"Who is he?" asked Connor, looking up from his calculator.

Joe shrugged.

"Well, is he complaining about something? Can't you deal with it?" Connor asked in exasperation.

"Not complaining, just wanted to speak to you."

Sighing, Connor took the stack of dollar bills he had been counting and put them in the safe.

"Tell him to come in, then."

Joe left the room, and moments later a young man, maybe a bit older than Connor himself, came into the room. He looked nervous, and strangely familiar.

"How can I help you?" Connor stood up behind the desk.

"Are you Connor Dean?" the man asked.

Connor's eyes widened as it occurred to him that this guy might have been sent to kill him. He was always watchful, ever mindful, of someone from back home who might be tracking him, and so far his luck had held.

"Who wants to know?" he asked roughly, taking a step back as the young man came up to the desk.

"My name's Ben. I think you might be my cousin."

It was the last thing that Connor had expected, and he sat back down with a jolt.

"Cousin?"

"Yes." Ben nodded eagerly. "My dad's David, he had a brother called Billy Dean. Is that your dad? Just a while ago he received a call from a lady named Mary, telling us that you were here and the reason why. Mary's your mom, right?"

"Yes, yes, she is." Connor grinned at the realisation that he now had his own family in New York. He stood up and shook Ben's outstretched hand. "God, it's good to meet you. Really, it is."

"Hey, man, you too!" Ben shook his hand with enthusiasm. "You gotta meet the rest of the family! They'll be thrilled that I found you."

"What about tonight? It's my birthday, and I'm having a meal with some friends at Le Cirque. Could you join us?"

"Sure, man. I'll see how many I can get together. We'll meet you there," Ben replied.

"About eight o'clock," Connor said. "And thanks for looking me up, Ben. You don't know what this means to me."

In her bedroom, Bronwyn stared in dismay at the array of clothes spread out on her bed. She had nothing suitable for dinner, nothing at all, and until now she hadn't realised how long it had been since she had got dressed up. In Crossmaglen she had been dressed to kill almost every night of the week, but there had been no need for that in New York. If she wasn't working, she was at home, with Connor, and there was no need for short skirts and high heels. Her panic grew as she realised that she didn't even have anything to wear for the christening tomorrow. Oh well, that meant up early for a trip to the mall. Thank God the shops here were open all weekend. That little crisis solved, Bronwyn turned her attention back to what to wear for tonight, sorting through the garments on the bed. Eventually she came up with a relatively smart pair of white trousers, with a matching white fitted suit jacket. She held it up and couldn't even remember buying it. Never mind, it would do. Now, just to find something to wear underneath. Putting the suit aside, she pulled open her drawers and flung yet more clothes onto the bed. Eventually she came up with a simple black vest and pulled it on. Her only pair of heels, strapless shoes with killer heels, and her outfit was complete. She stared critically in the mirror and raised an eyebrow. For an outfit thrown together, it wasn't bad.

Ten minutes later she came out of her room, just as Connor was coming through the door.

"Hey, you'll never guess—" He stopped abruptly when he saw her.

"What?" she asked anxiously. "Do I look stupid? I bloody knew it, Connor, I've nothing to wear!"

He shook his head and smiled.

"Its fine, you look…lovely," he said. "But, guess who I met today?"

Her eyes widened. "Someone famous?" she asked in awe.

"No, better than that!" he laughed. "I met my cousin, Ben."

"I didn't know you had a cousin here!" she exclaimed.

"Neither did I! Come with me while I get ready, and I'll tell you all about it."

She sat on his bed and listened while he told her about Ben's visit. She was delighted for him. It had been so very sad that Connor was here alone. At least she had some connection to her family through Cally. Now Connor had found a whole new family of his own. She checked out her reflection in the mirror, wanting to look her best to meet them all.

The meal was at Le Cirque, a restaurant on Madison Avenue where Sam had managed to acquire a table. As they walked in together, heads turned to look at Bronwyn. Connor noticed and was proud to be seen with her. He spotted Cally and Sam, and led Bronwyn over to their table.

About fifteen minutes later, the door of the restaurant opened and Connor squeezed Bronwyn's hand as he saw Ben come into the room. Ben wasn't alone; behind him trailed two women, two men and a young boy. Connor stood up and waved to Ben, and his family came over to the table.

"Everyone, this is Connor."

Connor was besieged by the sudden onset of attention that they all gave him, shaking the hands of the two men and returning the women's hugs warmly.

After they sat down and Ben had introduced everyone, Connor took a moment to study his new family.

There was Jean—Ben's mother—his aunt. She truly looked Irish, with her red hair and friendly green eyes. Her daughter, his cousin, Madeleine, was the same age as Connor. One of the two men was David, Connor's uncle, Billy's older brother. The other man, silent and carefully studying Connor, was Ray,

David's father. Connor was overwhelmed by the thought that not long ago he had thought that his life was forever ruined, and now here he was, in an exclusive restaurant in New York, on his birthday, sitting across the table from his grandfather.

"Who's this little lad?" he asked.

"This is William," Jean spoke up. "Billy, we call him. He's my youngest, and my last!"

"You named him for my dad," stated Connor and smiled at Jean. "Mum would be happy to hear that."

The meal was enjoyable, and they laughed at Connor as he made a mental note of some of the dishes to take back to Mayfair. After dessert, Sam and Cally handed Connor his gift and he took it eagerly. It was a flat package, and underneath the wrapping was an envelope. He ripped it open and held up the single piece of paper it contained. It seemed to be some sort of legal document, and he looked to Sam for an explanation.

"It's shares, shares in your name, for I.B.M. Trust me, Connor, this is really going to take off."

"Shares?" Bronwyn looked bemused.

"It's a portfolio," Sam explained. "You need to check these and, man, you just watch them rise. When they hit the roof, which they will, you cash in them sons of bitches and make a mint!" Sam, who played the stock market regularly, was excited and Cally put her head in her hands, shaking her head.

"That's so bloody boring!" she said. "Luckily, I got you something else."

She handed over a wrapped gift and Connor put the shares aside to open Cally's present. He pulled out a package, which was a very expensive aftershave; one that Bronwyn knew was his favourite.

"Thank you, *both* of you," he said and kissed Cally on the cheek.

Bronwyn put a small package on the table. He picked it up and unwrapped it slowly. It was a red box, and he smiled at Bronwyn before opening it. When he pulled off the lid his heart almost stopped in his chest. Nestled in the red velvet surround, was a bracelet. It was white gold, and so near to identical to the one that Rosina had given him on Christmas day, that he paled noticeably. The original one, Rosina's, had been left in Ireland in his haste to get away, and Bronwyn had never even known about its existence. He lifted it out and examined it. He saw markings on the inside and he asked Bronwyn what they were.

"It's Arabic. That's your name, there. That means 'friend', and that's my name. See?" She pointed it out and sat back, waiting for his reaction.

"It's beautiful. I love it," he said, slipping it on his wrist. "Thank you."

He leaned over, kissed her on her cheek, and sat back to admire his gift. It was beautiful, and he did love it; it reminded him of both Rosina and Bronwyn, and she would never know how much he would treasure it.

There were also gifts from Jean, David, Ray, Ben and little William, and Connor was touched.

"This really has been the best birthday," he said. "I'm so glad you're all here to share it with me. It makes it easier, because it stops me dwelling on the people who aren't here today."

Bronwyn swallowed the lump in her throat as she thought of Rosina, and Mary and Alia, Barry and Danny too. She picked up her glass and rose to stand next to Connor.

"A toast," she said. "To old friends, never forgotten, and new ones too."

Without saying anything, they clinked their glasses together. Seconds later, the laughter and chatter resumed until they noticed that they were the only diners left, and the restaurant staff were waiting patiently to close up for the night.

"Shall we call it a night? Big day tomorrow," said Sam as he called for the bill.

"Don't remind me. I've yet to buy something to wear," groaned Bronwyn.

Outside, Sam, Cally, Bronwyn and Connor said goodbye to the Deans, with promises to meet up with them very soon.

Then the four of them shared a taxi, Cally and Sam dropping them off on their way back to Manhattan. When Connor and Bronwyn got in, she flopped down on the couch.

"Coffee?" Connor called from the kitchen.

"Not for me. I should go to bed, seeing as I've got to be clothes shopping in the morning."

He came out into the room, holding two mugs, and she weakened.

"Oh, go on then."

With the coffee, they sat and caught up on each other's news of the past week and talked about Connor's new found family. When Bronwyn looked at the clock and saw it was past two in the morning, she squealed.

"Christ, look at the time! If I don't get up in the morning I'll blame you, Connor Dean!"

He laughed and stood up as she made her way to her room. He waited until she was at her doorway and called her name.

"Bronwyn!"

She turned around.

"Thanks for this." He held his hand up in the air, and she smiled and nodded.

"Goodnight."

The next morning, Bronwyn was out of the house before eight o'clock. The christening was at two, which left her five hours to buy something suitable to wear, and one hour to get ready. Plenty of time.

She took the subway into the heart of the city and wandered up and down the streets. Several times she passed Fifth Avenue, and when the time neared 11:30, she pulled out her credit card and looked at it. Fifth Avenue shopping was something that she couldn't afford, and her credit card was strictly for emergencies only. But as she looked once more at the time and thought of her unsuitable wardrobe back home, she put the card in her purse and turned into Fifth Avenue. If this wasn't an emergency, she didn't know what was. As she walked past the first store, Saks, a mannequin in the window caught her eye. The dress on the model was gorgeous. It was more than gorgeous; it was perfect. Before she could talk herself out of it, she went inside and asked the assistant who pounced on her if she could try it on.

Minutes later, in the changing room, she looked at her reflection and smoothed down the dress. It was a chiffon material, floor length with shoestring straps, and white in colour. It was almost fit for a bride except it was trimmed in silver, and as she admired the cut, she found herself wondering if Connor would like it.

"It's lovely, ma'am. It fits like it was made for you." Bronwyn let the assistant fawn over her and said she would take it.

It was four hundred dollars, more than anything she had ever paid for something to wear, but time was tight and she had to get home. On impulse, she added a small matte silver handbag and a pair of white high heels to her purchase and signed the six hundred dollar bill.

Hurrying home, she ran through the door. When she saw Connor, sitting on the window ledge, all dressed and ready to go, she ran past him into her room.

"Sorry...sorry, gimme ten minutes!" she called behind her, and Connor grinned to himself.

He was impressed when only twenty minutes later she came out of her room. He turned to look at her and stopped short. It had been so long since she had dressed up that the transformation shocked him. He thought that she had looked wonderful last night—almost daily he thought to himself how beautiful she was—but this, this was something else. The dress, which looked very expensive, skimmed over every curve and looked like it had been tailor made. Her jet-black hair was pinned up, with tendrils falling around her face.

"You're stunning," he said. Then he smiled and held out his arm.

"Shall we?"

She took his arm and smiled back at him.

"Let's go."

The service was emotional, mostly because Bronwyn knew Cally was thinking that her family should be here to witness her daughter's christening. Her own thoughts turned to the loved ones that she had lost; Barry, of whom there was still no news, Danny, and Rosina. As she looked around the church at Cally and Sam's friends and family, she realised that this was the way it should be. There were all sorts under the church roof this hot summer's day; Catholics, Protestants, Christians, Cally's neighbours who were Hindi, and Sam's funky black friend, Titus. All different races and religions, but they all had one thing in common; they all shared a love for Sam, Cally, and Bella. It was at that moment Bronwyn knew she had done the right thing in leaving Crossmaglen, to come to a land where everyone was free and accepted for what or who they were.

When the service was over and photographs had been taken, Connor made his way over to Bronwyn.

"Ready for the party?" he asked.

"You bet," she replied.

The party was being held in the grounds of the local football ground, and a live band was performing in the marquee that had been erected.

"I've got an idea," said Connor.

"What?"

"Let's get drunk." With that, he took her hand. Laughing, she followed him and the rest of the congregation a couple of blocks down the street to the party.

They did get drunk, because it had been a long time since they had been able to take the night off and enjoy themselves. They sat back in a corner of the room, laughing, while they drained the complimentary bottles of wine and enjoyed the food that had been laid out. Bronwyn thought she was going to have a coronary from giggling so hard when Connor was dragged off by Sam's aunt to dance. She watched him on the dance floor, thinking how good it was for him to let his hair down once in a while.

He may have changed quite a lot since their arrival in New York, she thought, but deep down he was still the same serious and sensitive Connor that she had fallen in love with.

She sat bolt upright and felt a flush spread over her. Now, why had she thought that? That she was in love with Connor had never entered her head before, and it sobered her considerably. She caught sight of the two empty wine bottles and felt relief flood through her. It was the drink talking, that was all. A few coffees and she'd be back to her sane way of thinking.

Suddenly Connor was at her side, flopping down into a chair and picking up his glass of wine.

"I'm having a nice time," he said, beaming at her.

"I'm glad. You should take more time out to enjoy yourself. It suits you," she replied.

The lights dimmed and the band switched tempo. A song came on, *As Time Goes By*, and Connor abandoned his glass of wine, pulling her to her feet. He turned quite serious before he pulled her towards him.

"May I have this dance?"

She glanced around the room, where all of the other couples were moving around to the song, nodded, and let him lead her onto the floor.

He spun her around and she laughed as he pulled her back in to him. He put his arms around her and held her very close. Liking the feeling of being in his arms, she wrapped her arms around him and put her head on his shoulder. Halfway through the song, she was aware that the mood seemed to have changed between them; they were no longer just friends having a laugh, this was something else. It was no one thing that made her feel this way, just the way he held her so tight, and how close his face was to hers. She closed her eyes, misery creeping up on her. Was this the way it was always going to be? Whenever she got close to him, wondering, wishing, thinking about what might have been, could have been...

He leaned away then, as if sensing her thoughts, and looked into her face. His eyes, so like hers, were dark and she swore she saw desire and longing in them. Was it real? Was it just wishful thinking, or maybe the wine that they had consumed? She leaned her head back on his shoulder, confused and perplexed.

"Bronwyn..." he whispered her name and she started, but didn't move her head off his shoulder.

"What?" she asked.

When he didn't answer she stopped moving and frowned at him. "Connor, what is it?"

He closed his eyes, paused and then forced out the words that he wanted to say.

"I'm in love with you." His tone was serious, and his words made her heart lurch.

She pulled back. He caught hold of her hands, preventing her from escaping and she looked up at him. He looked stunned, as if he couldn't believe he had said those words, and her surprised expression matched his.

It was what she had wanted to hear for months, but she had buried her feelings so deep that she had not allowed herself to think about it. But still...she had to be sure.

"You're drunk again," she stated.

"But happy drunk this time," he replied. "And right now, I feel quite sober."

It wasn't an answer; he sensed her apprehension and wondered what he could say to make her believe that his words were true. They had stopped moving, although by now the floor was so crowded that nobody took any notice of them.

"I want you all the time, everywhere, ever since I first met you; that never went away," he said, searching her face for a response. "Say it's all in my head, tell me you don't feel the same, and I'll never mention it again," he squeezed her hands. "*Do* you feel the same?"

"Yes," she uttered the word and it was as though a weight had been lifted off her shoulders, a weight that she had not even been aware of carrying.

They were quiet for a moment before Connor spoke up.

"Shall we go home?"

Less than thirty minutes later they stood in the lounge of the apartment, facing each other, both wary of this step that they were taking into unknown territory that would change everything for them. Bronwyn moved first, until she was close enough to touch him. She took his left hand in hers and kissed it. It was a signal, a green light, and Connor reached up with his right hand to brush the hair away from her face. He leaned in, closer, until their lips were touching, his hands coming up to pull her hair until it fell loose around her face. Suddenly, the passion hit them. There was a sense of urgency, as if they both realised this was what they had been waiting for, perhaps even before Rosina had died. The expensive dress, which Bronwyn had carried so carefully all the way home from Fifth Avenue, was now forgotten as it fell to the floor. Bronwyn pulled off his shirt. Unable to contain their hunger for each other any longer, they fell to the floor.

An hour later, they were both in the double bed in Bronwyn's room. Connor was asleep, so she took the chance to study him. He was so damn beautiful, she thought as she looked over his handsome face. His skin, naturally dark, had tanned to a deep bronze in the hot New York sun. His body was muscled, his chest smooth and brown. Her eyes traveled down his body and she stared at the scar that marked his leg. It had healed well, and although he walked with a slight limp, it was barely noticeable. She looked back up at his face. He was smiling slightly in his sleep, and she felt a flutter in the pit of her stomach at the thought of him in *her* bed. She couldn't believe that it had finally happened, that he had said he *loved* her, and she offered up a short prayer that he wouldn't regret it come morning. His eyes slowly opened and he looked at her sleepily, propped up on one elbow, sheet clutched tightly to her, watching over him.

"Hey," he murmured, holding out his arms.

Happily, she lay down beside him, and they lay encircled in each other's arms until dawn, two kindred spirits, who had finally found each other in the best way of all.

Connor opened his eyes and for a second the unfamiliar room confused him. Then he remembered and he sat up, looking over at Bronwyn's side of the bed. She wasn't there, so he climbed out of the bed and wandered through to the lounge. She was standing with her back to him, looking out the window, sipping from a bottle of water.

"Hi," he said and she turned around.

"Morning," she replied. "How are you?"

"Fine."

He frowned. They were being awfully polite. He hoped that she wasn't regretting last night. He couldn't stand it if their friendship was ruined.

He walked over to her and decided honesty was the best option here. Speaking from his heart, he laid his cards on the table.

"I've no regrets, Bronwyn. I know you, and I can see you're wondering." He took her hand. "I've wanted you for so long that I'm really scared of messing up. I don't want to ruin things between us."

"You know I feel the same," she said, turning back to the window. "I can't help but think about…"

"Rosie?" he finished for her and she nodded.

"Bron, Rosina was so special, but…it wasn't right between us."

It was the first time that Connor had admitted it to himself, and he felt something like betrayal towards Rosina as he said the words.

"What do you mean? You two were perfect together," Bronwyn exclaimed. She led Connor over to the table and pulled up a chair beside him.

"My ma, she asked me if I was in love with Rosina—if there was passion, and fire, and all that." Connor's face burned with embarrassment. "There wasn't. I know that now. I even knew it then." He looked up at Bronwyn, shaking his head sadly. "I'd never met someone so good, so pure, sweet, and innocent—all I wanted to do was protect her."

"Oh, Connor." She laid her hand over his, not knowing what else to say.

"Then there was you, so confident, so outspoken and brave, and from the start I could see that you'd been protecting her all her life as well. And what I feel for you is so, so different." He gripped her hand tightly. "Should I feel guilty?"

She pulled him into an embrace.

"No," she whispered. "There are so many different kinds of love, Connor. The way you feel about me now doesn't mean that you loved Rosie any less. You just loved her in a different way."

She felt him relax against her, the tension flowing from his body, and he held her tight.

"Thank you," he whispered.

* * * *

Across the street from their apartment, a solitary figure sat in a coffee shop and stared up into Connor and Bronwyn's window. The man had been sitting there for over an hour now, watching Bronwyn as she sat in the window, lost in her own thoughts. When Connor appeared behind her, and they exchanged words before holding each other close, a small smile played on the man's lips. He was glad that the couple was happy and had found each other; it had certainly taken enough time. He hoped that they took advantage of every minute they spent together, because life was precious, as he had found out for himself.

The man, sitting alone, nursing a single cup of coffee that was now cold, got up and, throwing some coins on the table, left the shop to make his way down to the set of three telephone booths at the corner of the block. Minutes later, the middle telephone began to ring. He stepped inside and picked up the receiver.

"Hello?"

"It's me," the familiar voice came from the end of the line. "It's starting, so keep your head down and it'll all be over soon. Have you seen them?"

"Yes. Just now." The man nodded. "They're at home."

"Good. There's a telephone booth covered with graffiti on the far corner of Times Square. Be there tomorrow at six P.M., and I should be able to call you with good news."

He hung up and left the telephone booth. One more day— just one more day. He had to hold on and keep watch on Bronwyn and Connor, then he could make his presence known.

* * * *

Later, when Bronwyn and Connor had got out of bed for the second time, they sat opposite each other at the kitchen table and talked about what was happening between them.

"I thought it was just me. I never thought you were interested," admitted Bronwyn.

"We wasted so much time," replied Connor.

Bronwyn thought about it and shook her head. The timing was wrong before, she told Connor, both of them had been too shattered by events in their lives to embark on a relationship. Friendship was what they had needed then, and now that they were stable, the time was right.

"Cally will be pleased," she said, giggling. "She said you were mad about me."

"Cally is a very perceptive lady. Why don't we stop by there later? We did leave the party without saying goodbye," he said.

"You're right. I'm sure she'll understand, but we'll drop in," she looked at him coyly. "Are you not going to work today?"

"No, I'm not." He pulled her up from her chair and onto his lap. "Today I've much more important things to do."

Chapter Sixteen

Endings

Back in Crossmaglen, after a long period without trouble, tensions were rising in the army barracks. Stu sat up in the observation tower, literally counting the hours down until the end of his shift. Tonight was his last shift—his last ever day in Crossmaglen, and he was more than ready to go home. Home to his family, and to Ellie. He knew that when he arrived home he had a lot of thinking to do about his future in the army, or whether he wanted to continue in this career. He was almost certain that he didn't; after the two easy years in England, Northern Ireland had changed him for the worse, and he didn't want to risk being sent somewhere similar to Ireland, where the depression would take further hold of him. It hadn't all been bad though. He would take away some memories of this town and hold them to him for the rest of his life. Bronwyn was one of these memories that he thought about every so often, on his shifts in the tower. He hadn't known her well, but he would have liked to, and he hoped wherever she was now she was happy. Surprisingly, he had kept in contact with Alia, who had introduced him to Mary, the mother of the lad who had been with Bronwyn that fateful night. The army would have no doubt frowned upon his fraternising with the enemy. That's what they were, technically. Both women visited him occasionally, normally bringing him some homemade food or a bottle of alcohol. With Bronwyn gone, these two had made his life in Crossmaglen sane, and he would always be grateful for that. In fact, he decided, he would go visit Alia when he came off shift, to say goodbye to her. That decided, he called Carter up into the tower and persuaded him to play a hand of cards with him.

* * * *

Kathleen James, Rosina's mother, was in the dark depths of despair, and had been since Rosina had died. It was more true to say she had felt this sadness since Rosina was conceived, but until she had told her daughter the truth, she had managed to keep the depression at bay. Now it ate away at her, gnawing her from inside out, and if the truth were told, Kathleen was slowly going crazy. She blamed the bastard man who had ruined her life almost twenty-two years ago, but because she had no chance of finding him, she had nobody to vent her frustration on. If only Rosina hadn't gone off with the Protestant; that had been the undoing of them. If she'd just left well alone, they would have continued muddling along together and she wouldn't be dead.

Kathleen sat and thought about it, in the large house that was now too big for just one person. It had been days since she had eaten anything. Even when she did force some food down, it was mere morsels, but she didn't care. The Prozac her doctor had given her, washed down with a quart of gin every day, was all she needed to keep afloat. But now the pills weren't working, it had all become too much, and Kathleen knew that she was not much longer for this earth. One way or another, be it by the pills and alcohol, or the hand of God, she was nearing the end of her time on this earthly plane, and for that Kathleen was grateful. But before she went, there was something she had to do, and she was trying to get up the courage to go there now. She needed her revenge. Because the father of her child and Connor were nowhere to be found, she would wreak havoc on the next person in line, the woman who had stolen her girl away from her.

Mary Dean.

* * * *

Alia sat in Mary's kitchen and waited until Mary had opened the bottle of wine and poured out two glasses before she told her the news.

"Come on then." Mary sat down. "You're like a cat on a hot tin roof!"

"Bronwyn called me this morning. She's found herself a boyfriend."

"Well, fancy that. American?" Mary asked as she sipped at her wine.

"No, Irish…" She raised her eyebrows at Mary and waited for the penny to drop.

"My boy?" Mary threw back her head and laughed. "Well, it's about bloody time!"

"That's what I said," replied Alia. "And she said that Connor's met up with your husband's family. That's real good news."

Mary smiled; she was very pleased that she had tracked down Billy's family in New York. It had taken some work; there had been none of his family in Crossmaglen to ask. She had gone back to Billy's old neighbourhood and asked around. They all remembered her. They also remembered what had happened to Billy, therefore most of them were unwilling to help her. But eventually she had found an elderly neighbour who still sent Christmas cards to Billy's brother, David, and she had willingly passed over his address in America.

"He wasn't my husband," she said, smiling sadly. "But it's nice to hear him called that."

"It must have been very hard," said Alia. "Losing him like that."

Mary was just about to reply when there was a knock on the back door.

"It's open," Mary called out and they both turned to see who their visitor was.

"Just me." Stu came into the kitchen. "It's my last day, and I just wanted to say goodbye. I went to your place, Alia, but figured you'd be here."

"Come in. Take a glass of wine with us."

Mary, like Alia, had grown fond of the English boy who seemed to have attached himself to them. Since Connor and Barry, the men of the families, had gone, he had tried to make sure that they were both okay, and both the women appreciated that.

"I've got something for you." Stu pulled a Smith & Wesson revolver out of his bag and put it on the table.

The two women stared at it.

"Bloody hell," said Alia.

"Listen, we've got intelligence back in the barracks. They tell us stuff that they hear and, believe me, things are getting worse. I want you to keep this here, but it never came from me, okay?" Stu said.

"I don't know if I could use it," Mary said. "And if I did, I'd probably miss."

"It doesn't matter if you don't use it. If someone came after you, pointing it at them would be enough."

"Show us how to use it," Alia said.

Twenty minutes later the gun was lying partially dismantled in Stu's lap. He was satisfied that the women had a basic knowledge on how to use the weapon, and now he allowed himself to relax, helping himself to a glass of wine to mark the end of his service in Crossmaglen.

As he chatted with Alia and Mary, he caught sight of a shape moving past the kitchen window. He was just about to ask Mary if she was expecting anybody, when the back door crashed open. The three seated at the table gaped at the woman standing in the doorway.

It was Kathleen; she was drunk, trying to stand steady, leaning on the frame of the door for support. Her eyes were wild, and she looked a million miles away from the poised woman that Alia had known. The thing that scared Alia most, though, was the large, shiny gun that sprouted from her hands, pointed straight towards Mary.

"Kathleen…" Alia went to stand up and Kathleen immediately swung the gun in her direction.

Alia sat down abruptly, and Kathleen turned once more to face Mary.

"You took my girl," she said, in an eerily calm voice.

Mary stared back at the woman whom she had never met but had heard so much about.

"She came to me. You threw her out," she replied defiantly.

As soon as Kathleen had burst into the room, gun in hand, Stu had started to reassemble the revolver that lay in his lap. He did it, stealthily and silently, calling upon all of his experiences with firearms to help him regain control of this situation. Now, with the revolver together and fully operational, he slid off the safety catch, and the click echoed in the silent room. Kathleen, drunk as she was, heard it and looked at him as if noticing him for the first time. He stood up, and as he did so she saw the glint of metal in his hand. Almost on reflex, she moved the handgun across to him at the same time as he held up the Smith & Wesson. Stu tried to shout, to tell her to be calm and put her gun down, but when he saw her finger squeeze the trigger, he knew he had no choice but to let off a shot of his own.

Shoot to wound, he told himself, *not to kill*, and he angled the gun down slightly.

A huge noise erupted from Kathleen's rifle, and Alia let out a scream. The shot was amazingly accurate, catching Stu in his stomach before he could get a shot of his own off, and he fell backwards, reaching behind to try to remain standing. Another shot rang out and caught him in his left thigh. He let out a yell between clenched teeth and slipped down the wall, where he flailed around on the floor, trying to breathe, trying to get the pain under control. Holding his right arm steady with his left, he pulled up his hand and aimed the gun at her. Not caring now if he killed the mad woman, he let off three shots in quick succession, knowing that he had to hit her *now*, because he wouldn't be able to hold on much longer.

The kitchen was filled with smoke, and when it cleared a little he saw the woman again. She was on the floor, writhing around and making odd noises in the back of her throat that told him he had hit her well; the bullets had ripped through her chest, and she was choking on the blood that filled her lungs. Seeing that his job was done, he moved his head around to his left and tried to focus his gaze on Alia and Mary. They were crouched on the floor, arms around each other and heads down. They were all right, he thought with relief, and let his gun drop to the floor. It was getting harder and harder to catch his breath. He laid his head back to lean against the wall. He held on until he could hear nothing more from the dead woman in front of him, and then his head fell forward.

His job was done.

It was over.

* * * *

231

"Someone's been following me," said Bronwyn, as they sat in Mayfair.

The bar was empty, all the customers had left, and Bronwyn was helping Connor to clear up before he locked up for the night. Now, as she made the statement that she was being followed, he frowned and automatically glanced out of the window into the street.

"What do you mean?" he asked.

She put the final glasses in the dishwasher and turned to face him over the bar.

"The last few weeks, it's like someone's watching me."

"Well, who is it?" he asked.

"I don't know. I've not seen anyone. It's just a weird feeling. Like I'm walking down the street and I sense someone watching, but when I turn around, nobody's there," she struggled to explain. She wondered if Connor thought she was overreacting, but when she looked at him he looked concerned.

"I don't want you going anywhere on your own," he said. "You know I'm always going to have to be careful. People from back home might still be after me. From now on, you're not to be alone anywhere, okay?"

She nodded, relieved he didn't think she was a basket case. Glancing around the bar, she realised that although it was late, she wasn't tired, and didn't feel like going home yet.

"Wanna stay here awhile?" she asked. "I can make us some food in the kitchen."

Connor nodded and watched her as she went into the kitchen. When she was gone, he walked over to the front windows and looked out into the street. People walked past, hurrying along to wherever they were going. Nobody was loitering or looking suspicious. He came back to the bar and sat down. If someone was following Bronwyn, they would have to get through him first.

* * * *

The night of 11th July, 1981, was one that the residents of Crossmaglen would never forget. In years to come, stories of the night's events would be told, and would become as infamous as some of the other attacks that places around the world had suffered at the hands of the I.RA. The troubles began in two separate spots, the army barracks and the local government offices, and quickly spread throughout most of the town. Alia and Mary missed all of it, for they were in the safest place − the R.U.C police station about a mile from Mary's house. They were being interviewed, separately, about what had happened in Mary's kitchen earlier in the evening.

The first batch of explosives went off outside the army base at nine o'clock. They had been cleverly made, and cunningly concealed, as the perpetrators hid in the woods surrounding the perimeter of the camp. None of the soldiers even knew that they were there.

The seventy soldiers who were there were supposed to be prepared for an attack. Intelligence had been received, but even they did not know when the attack was going to happen. Only the most loyal I.R.A members had been let in on the date and time. The first casualty of the night was Tracker, the barracks' faithful Alsatian dog. As he walked around the camp, nose to the ground, sniffing for hidden explosives as he had been trained to, the first bomb exploded, tearing the dog apart like a hot knife through butter. The soldiers, hearing his howl just as clearly as they heard the explosion, raced into action. Suddenly all hell broke loose, as all other fourteen bombs exploded around the edge of the camp and the sky lit up as though it was the 5th of November. Carter, knowing that this was going to be a massive attack, picked up the phone in the observation tower to call for back up. He stared dumbly at the receiver as he realised the phone line was dead. He picked up the other two phones and got the same response. Running over to the window overlooking the gates of the camp, he peered outside and was panicked by what he saw; twenty, maybe thirty men flooding through the gates and broken fences, armed to the hilt with machine guns and sawn-off shotguns. He kicked the hatch shut and locked it, before resuming his position by the window and fumbling for the C.B. radio to call for help. It was going to be a very long night.

* * * *

At 1 A.M., New York time, a man stood alone by the set of telephone booths in the corner of Times Square. He gazed continuously around him, pulling the collar of his leather jacket up to conceal his face. At 1:04 a telephone began to ring. The man threw down the cigarette he had been smoking and stepped into the booth. He cast one more furtive glance over his shoulder, and picked up the telephone.

"Hello?"

"It's me. You doing okay?"

"Yes." The man gripped the receiver tightly. "Tell me."

"It's all over. We got our men, now you can go and get yours."

The line went dead in his ear, and the man held onto the receiver for a moment longer. Eventually, he hung up the telephone and stepped back outside. He looked across the square, into the windows of Mayfair, and saw the lone figure of Connor as he moved around the restaurant, picking up empty bottles and depositing them on the bar. The man's mouth twitched into a smile, and he started to walk towards the restaurant, picking up his pace as he moved across the square, until he was almost running.

Bronwyn had just picked up their empty plates off the table when the outer door to the restaurant was pushed open.

"You didn't lock it?" Connor asked, standing up.

"I thought you did," she said. "Go tell them we're closed, and lock the door."

"Hey, we're closed, buddy," called Connor, as a man opened the second set of doors that led into the bar.

"I'm here to see Bronwyn," the man replied.

Bronwyn looked up at the familiar Irish twang.

The man who had asked for her was standing in the shadows of the door and as he walked further into the bar, her hand flew to her mouth.

"Hi," he said. "It's been a long time."

She tried to reply, but found that speech was impossible. She breathed hard, blinking to make sure that she wasn't imagining it. Connor moved next to her and touched her arm.

"Bronwyn?" he asked, concerned.

"Barry!" suddenly she could talk, and she screamed with joy. "It's *Barry*!"

She ran to him, throwing her arms around his neck, and he spun her around the room, joining in her delight.

"Where have you been? Oh, God, it's so good to see you." She began to cry, great heaving sobs. Barry pulled her close and felt a tear trickle down his face.

She could tell that his emotions were as highly charged as hers, it was the longest they had ever been apart and for a long moment they stayed enveloped in each other's arms.

Eventually, Bronwyn remembered Connor, and pulled away from Barry.

"Barry, this is Connor. You remember him, don't you?"

Barry walked over to Connor, Bronwyn still hanging on his arm, and shook his hand.

"We never met, but I remember," Barry said. "How're you doing?"

"Uh, I'm fine. It's good to finally meet you at last," replied Connor, liking the look of Barry straight away.

Bronwyn moved over to Connor and linked her arm through his.

"I'm with Connor now," she said.

"I know. I was sorry about Rosina," Barry said.

Bronwyn frowned and exchanged a glance with Connor.

"How do you know? About us I mean? Have you been in touch with Ma?"

"Not yet." Barry sat down at one of the tables and pulled out a cigarette. "Do you mind if I smoke?"

"Go ahead," Connor was amused. "It *is* a bar."

Bronwyn pulled a chair out and sat down opposite Barry.

"How did you know about me and Connor?"

"I've been here a while, but I couldn't make contact before tonight," he said.

"I knew someone was following me. I said, didn't I, Connor?" she was immensely relieved it had been Barry, and not someone else from back home with a grudge against Connor. "But, why couldn't you see me before now? And where have you been all this time?"

Barry lit up his cigarette and pondered her question. He thought about where he had been for the last six months, and wondered how much to tell her. After a few moments of silence, he decided to tell her the whole story.

When he had left Banbridge house on New Year's Day, it was already dark. He left on foot, his mind clear for the first time in weeks, and he knew that he had to get away. If he stayed in Banbridge they would only do so many more tests, and then just declare him fit, not suffering from anything other than a nervous breakdown, and send him home. If he went home, he would be killed. It had broken his heart that he couldn't tell anyone where he was going, but at least that way his mother and Bronwyn wouldn't have to lie for him. He made his way to Belfast Airport and withdrew all of his money from the cash point machine. As he stood in the middle of the bustling airport, he realised that he needed help in getting away. He had planned nothing more than leaving Banbridge, and now that he had managed to do that, he had no idea what his next move would be. He made his way to a telephone box and dialed Johnny's number, hoping that the man would stick to his end of the agreement that they had made; if Barry were ever in trouble because of his job, they would protect him. Johnny was true to his word, and he told Barry exactly what to do.

"Stay there and wait by the phone. Give me the number."

Barry had reeled the number off and hung up the phone.

Less than an hour later, Johnny called back and told Barry to go to the Air Lingus desk and collect his ticket; it had been bought and paid for. Barry asked where he was going. Johnny told him Canada.

So Barry went to Canada. Montreal, in fact, and when he landed it was cold and snowing. He stayed there for four months, living in the Hyatt hotel, all paid for by the British government. The insomnia that had haunted him had not left, but it had not worsened either, and Barry was gradually coming to terms with getting just four or so hours of sleep each night. He stayed in constant contact with Johnny, telling him repeatedly that he had to get out of there, to see Bronwyn, speak to his mother. Johnny told him it was impossible. Eventually, on the first of May, Barry told Johnny that he'd had enough; he was leaving to go to New York to be with Bronwyn. Johnny, perhaps sensing his determination, relented. He could go, but he couldn't see her, not yet.

"Why?" Barry had demanded.

"She's being watched. So is the boy she's with. They're being shadowed the whole time, and not by us."

Barry's blood had run cold; it was *them*, and now they were after Bronwyn.

"But we're onto them. We're pulling the plug on the whole operation, and when those high up have gone, the people in New York will disappear."

Barry had to take his word; trust was all he had now. Johnny had been right, for on 11th July, today, the agents had hijacked the attack that had been planned, both in New York and in Northern Ireland. Now, as Barry sat and told his story to Bronwyn and Connor, the death count in Crossmaglen had begun to rise.

Bronwyn and Connor looked at Barry.

Barry stared back.

"What about Ma?" said Bronwyn fearfully.

"I need to call her. Crossmaglen was a war zone tonight, and I need to make sure she wasn't caught in any crossfire," he replied.

Bronwyn stood up and pulled Barry to the phone.

"Ring her," she instructed. She left him at the phone and drifted back over to Connor.

"Are you okay?" he asked.

"I will be, when I know that Ma's all right," she said.

"She'll have been with my mam, you'll see. They'll both be fine."

"Yes," said Bronwyn, looking back over at Barry.

How strange it was to see him again. He had changed; he had always seemed to be under a cloud in Ireland, fearful in a way. He looked healthier, stronger, and she had no doubt that if he stayed with her and Connor in New York, he would be happier as well. Now he could stay; he no longer had to hide away. Now he had beaten them, they had all beaten them, and gone on to rebuild their lives. She smiled to herself. She was proud of them all.

As Barry came back to the table, his face was pale. Bronwyn clutched at his hand, a worried expression springing to her face.

"Ma's been at the police station all night."

"Why?"

"She was at Mary's." He looked at Connor. "Rosina's mother tried to kill her."

"Who?" Connor and Bronwyn shouted at the same time.

"Mary."

"Christ alive!" Connor stood up, grabbing Barry in a blind panic. "Is she okay?"

"Yes, it's weird though." Barry sat down, a puzzled look on his face.

"What? Tell us Barry!" Bronwyn cried.

"Ma was with Mary, and they had this soldier there. Apparently they saw a lot of him since we all left. He kind of made a point of making sure they were all right. He was there, and he killed Kathleen when she came in. She was armed."

For a second Bronwyn was confused. And then it clicked.

"Stu Jackson," she whispered.

"You knew him?" Barry asked.

239

"Yeah, well, sort of. He was good to me—helped me out more than once when I got in trouble." She looked up suddenly. "You said Kathleen was armed. Is Stu okay?"

Barry frowned before shaking his head. "He's dead."

Bronwyn nodded, as if it had been what she was expecting. Twice he had saved her, both times from Danny. Now he had saved her mother—and Mary too, and had paid the ultimate price.

Silently she thanked him, wherever he was now, and she knew that he was one person she would never forget.

* * * *

Mary and Alia made their way to New York in the late summer of 1981 to join the rest of their families in Manhattan. By Christmas, they had all settled into their respective homes; Alia and Barry sharing a brownstone on Park Avenue, and Mary, not too far away on 34th Street, in a small apartment overlooking Central Park.

Mary had been delighted to meet Billy's family. They welcomed her with open arms, Jean especially. She was moved, and touched, as they told her stories of Billy from his youth. It was like getting to know him, properly this time, even though he was no longer with them.

Life went on for Connor and Bronwyn, without Rosina, Danny, Stu, and Kathleen, just like it had gone on for Mary and Cally. Although they would never forget their loved ones, it got a little easier each day, just like Cally had told Connor it would.

Chapter Seventeen

The End

It was spring in New York, four years later, when Connor received the telephone call from Sam that he had been waiting for, summoning him to his office down town.

Connor arrived at Sam's building within the hour. Sam was waiting, a huge stack of papers on his desk, and a big grin on his face.

"Sit down," he said, pushing a piece of paper across the desk towards Connor.

Connor turned the paper around and looked at it. It had a figure written on it in bold black pen.

"What's this?" Connor asked.

"It's your dream about to become a reality." Sam smiled.

Connor slumped back in his chair. For two years he and Bronwyn had worked alongside Sam trying to get investors to put together a sum of money that was enough to open their own bar. Every cent they had earned after rent had gone into the 'Dream Pot'. Their family had joined in their dream, all working towards finally making something good happen in their lives. Now, as Sam said, it was no longer a dream, but reality.

Six months later...

Once they had enough money to invest in their very own business venture, things moved very quickly. They looked for a suitable site, and came up with a derelict building on Park

Avenue, near Oscar's restaurant and just a couple of blocks away from Alia's new home. It was in bad shape, in need of serious work, but it was cheap and Connor put a deposit down the same day. Now, as Connor stood with Bronwyn in front of the newly decorated building, he thought back to the day that they had sat inside and tried to think of a name fitting for their venue.

"Okay, so a name...any thoughts?" Connor asked as he sat down at one of the new tables.

"Yeah, what about you?" Bronwyn replied.

Connor nodded, and put his closed notepad on the table.

Bronwyn pulled a sheet of paper out of her pocket and held it to her chest.

"You go first," she said.

Connor hesitated for a moment before opening the book and putting it face up on the table. She read what was written there, before raising her eyes to meet his.

"What do you think?" he asked anxiously.

"I think that great minds think alike," she said, and put her piece of paper on top of his notebook.

They had both chosen the same name, and although it should have, it didn't really surprise Connor. For him, and for her it seemed, it had been an obvious choice.

Now it was the grand opening, and Connor stood, savoring the moment. It was nearly dark, or as dark as it got in the brightly-lit city of New York, and quite a crowd had assembled. Alia and Mary, Barry, Sam, Cally and Bella waiting in anticipation, along with Lucia from Zak's, employees from Mayfair, Jean, David, Madeleine, Ben, and little Billy.

Connor stood at the entrance to the building next to Bronwyn. He took her hand and turned to face his friends and family.

"As you know, Bronwyn and I left our home with nothing. We were made welcome here by all of you that are here tonight. We found people willing to give us jobs and a place to stay; we found friends, and we discovered family that we never knew. It's with thanks to all of you, your money, time, hard work and support, that we are able to realise our dream here tonight." He squeezed Bronwyn's hand and she flicked the switch, standing back as the front of the building was illuminated. Neon lights, scrawled across the front of the building, spelled out the name of their new bar:

Rosie's.

About The Author

Jeanette has completed five manuscripts and is mid-way through a sixth.

She has worked with The Front List, which is a website with the aim of allowing their community of writers to self-select promising work by providing detailed feedback in the form of a critique. She has also had a short story accepted which appeared in the December 2007 edition of the Jimston Journal. Most recently Jeanette won silver prize in the Author V Author Short Story competition 2008 which was supported by the National Literacy Trust.

Author photo by East Coast Photography

Lightning Source UK Ltd.
Milton Keynes UK
UKOW04f0638240116

266957UK00001B/2/P